For my mother Ann and in memory of my father Timothy.

Acknowledgements

And so at the beginning I have come to the end. Though these are the first lines of *Consuming Passions*, I have approached them last. But I would not have reached this point were it not for an invaluable group of people who advised, encouraged, calmed and soothed.

I would like to thank Bernardine and Aengus Dewar for researching and testing many of the recipes and Bernardine for her editorial suggestions.

My grateful thanks go to Robin Coope, Tadgh Geary, Brendan and Lucinda O'Sullivan, Loretta Glucksman, James Donnelly, Catherine Carney, Lisa Murphy, Declan Ryan (for his invaluable help with the wines) and Bill Conliffe who took the cover photograph in Hydra.

Both staffs at Blackwater Press and at the *Sunday Independent* have been a constant source of support and help and while it is invidious to single people out, I am particularly grateful to John O'Connor and to Anne Harris for their vigorous enthusiasm and rigorous standards, both of which have influenced the shaping of this book.

I also wish to express my gratitude to all the friends who parted with precious recipes and who are mentioned in the book. It was especially (and characteristically) generous of Julie Campbell who is writing her own cookery book.

All my life people have been asking me, 'When's the book coming out?' This might not have been quite what they were expecting but they (and I) have Michael O'Sullivan to thank for talking me into undertaking the whole task.

And so I pen the last few words of my first book and appropriately come to my family, first and last at all times in my life. I've been thankful to them for decades for the depth of their love and loyalty. They never waver, and are unflinching in the face of my demands which recently, with deadlines snapping at my (Stephane Kélian) heels, have been unusually frenetic. They have, as ever, my deepest thanks, my profoundest love.

Contents

Introduction

If you've got this far, it's probably because curiosity got the better of you and you asked yourself, 'What does that one know about cookery?' Even close friends tried to contain their merriment when I opened the champagne to celebrate signing the contract. After all Terry, they pointed out, you don't make dinner, you make reservations.

Eaten tomato and fennel bread is soon forgotten and how quickly they forgot my decade spent as a cookery writer for a national paper and the two years I toiled as restaurant critic for the *Sunday Independent*. And that's only the professional side of my life. I've spent half a century eating, drinking and carousing in the best restaurants in the world. All my friends are superlative cooks and if they're not, they are married to them.

I will admit that I'm more at home in the dining-room than the kitchen and I would never be stirring a sauce when I could be shaking a martini. But I love cooking and appreciate good food. I cook to impress and as an indefatigable hostess I haven't poisoned anyone yet.

There are over a hundred recipes between these covers but like its writer, there's more to this book than meets the eye. It's about travel and parties and friends and places. It's about the fun (and the food) I've had and the people I love. So I don't want to end up gathering grease on a kitchen shelf. I want you to take me to bed with you. I know it won't be everyone's cup of Lapsang, but for those of you who have a keen appetite for life, I hope my book enriches and enhances it further.

Restorative Breakfasts & Blissful Brunches

'My wife and I tried to breakfast together but we had to stop or our marriage would have been wrecked.'
Winston Churchill.

Winston was right about matrimony and marmalade not mixing well. As Oscar Wilde said, only dull people are brilliant at breakfast, but an agreeable companion can be conducive to enjoyment and though, in theory, the best breakfasts are consumed alone some of my happiest memories are with the undemanding types who don't mind me reading a newspaper or eating in silence.

For me, memorable breakfasts depend mostly on location and people rather than grub. The view is vital, be it the Paris skyline seen from the terrace of the Meurice's white penthouse, the dramatic silhouette of Table Mountain from the Mount Nelson or the soothing sight of Lake Como lapping the shore from the Villa D'Este.

It would be hard to improve on my simple Parisian breakfast in the Café de la Madeleine with its comforting *café au lait* and the best croissants in town. My healthiest breakfasts were in Oaxaca, where Justine and I used to start the day with huge platters of exotic fruit, washed down with watermelon juice.

Of course there are days when a girl needs radical reconstruction before she can face food of any description. My own morning-after formula is to get into the shower, wash my hair and mix a bullshot. This is a fine, nourishing drink designed mainly for survival and restoration. They are probably the most effective, and certainly the most tolerable, hair of the dog ever invented. Although they are made in the best bars all over the world the bullshot's natural habitat is the Oak Bar in the Plaza Hotel in New York. They also serve an elegant version in the Plaza Athénée in Paris.

As soon as the sun crosses the yard-arm the time for a bullshot is nigh. If neither sun nor yard-arm is readily available settle for the crack of noon. Kipling's words:

> 'There are nine and sixty ways
> Of constructing tribal lays
> And every single one of them is right.'

could just as easily be applied to bullshots but here is my own, definitive formula. (For those in need of even more urgent treatment there is also the Prairie Oyster.)

THE KEANE BULLSHOT

With as steady a hand as you can achieve, reach for the cocktail shaker. For each imbiber combine:

2 measures of the best duck or game consomée you can get.

1 measure of pepper or lemon-flavoured Russian vodka, such as Pestrovska but plain Stolichnaya will do. Good vodka should always be kept in the freezer, where it acquires that lovely oily texture. (This also means that you don't have to add any ice cubes.)

4 dashes of Worcester sauce.

$1/_2$ tsp celery salt.

3 good squeezes of a fresh, juicy lemon.

Put all these ingredients in the shaker and shake vigorously – a screw-topped glass jar will do for this function, but remember to leave some space to allow for the shaking.

A frothy white collar on the drink is part of the mystique so shake until you have this.

Pour reverently into a handsome glass.

THE PRAIRIE OYSTER

1 measure cognac

The yolk of a raw egg

A good dash of Worcester sauce

A pinch of cayenne pepper

Mix the cognac and the seasonings together in a shot glass then drop in the raw egg yolk, whole.

Swallow in a single gulp.

After a few moments you should be feeling sufficiently able to enjoy the delicious breakfast and brunch dishes that follow.

Brunch is the most luxurious and leisurely of meals and one of my favourite places to have it is in London's Le Caprice on a Sunday. My to-die-for brunch choice there, is always Eggs Benedict, a jug of Bloody Mary and fresh berries with unwhipped cream. Tim Hughes, the head chef kindly gave me his recipe.

LE CAPRICE EGGS BENEDICT WITH HASH BROWNS
serves 4

4 muffins

8 eggs

4 slices of kassler bacon (or smoked bacon)

¼ pint hollandaise sauce

Hash browns to garnish

1 shallot, chopped

¼ pint white wine vinegar

¼ pint white wine

1 sprig tarragon, chopped

1 sprig thyme, chopped

½ bay-leaf

2 egg yolks

2 oz clarified butter

TO ASSEMBLE THE DISH:

Cut the muffins in half and toast.

Grill the bacon and place on the toasted muffin halves with a poached egg on top of each slice of bacon.

Cover with warm hollandaise sauce and garnish with hash browns.

TO MAKE THE HOLLANDAISE:

Reduce the vinegar, wine, herbs and chopped shallot by cooking gently in a saucepan.

Put the egg yolks in a bowl and whip them until the texture is light and fluffy.

Gradually beat in the hot wine and vinegar mixture and then the warm, clarified melted butter.

1 egg white, lightly beaten

2 onions

4 large potatoes cooked in their skins

1½ oz potato flour

Celery salt

Freshly ground white pepper and oil for frying

TO MAKE THE HASH BROWNS:

Slice and sweat the onions in butter until well-cooked but not browned.

Skin and grate the potatoes.

Combine the onions, potatoes and seasoning together.

Shape into balls with a teaspoon, coat in egg white, then dust with potato flour.

Fry in hot oil.

The Russian Tea Rooms in New York is another great brunch venue. Their Blinis *au caviar* are so addictive that I used to have withdrawal symptoms until June Levine saved me with this recipe for buckwheat blinis.

BLINIS

(makes 2 dozen)

5 oz buckwheat flour (available in health food shops)

½ tsp salt

3 oz plain white flour

½ tsp sugar

½ pint milk

1 packet dried yeast

¼ pint sour cream

3 eggs, separated

2 oz melted butter

Mix all the dry ingredients together.

Heat the milk until it is at blood heat (test the temperature on the inside of your wrist).

Make a well in the centre of the dry ingredients and pour in the milk.

Mix to a smooth batter then cover and leave in a warm room or a very low oven until it doubles in volume. This should take between 1 and 1½ hours. Do not leave it too long or it will turn sour.

Beat it well then add the sour cream, egg yolks and melted butter. (The butter will prevent the batter from sticking.)

Cover again and leave for a further 30 minutes. Meantime whip the egg-whites until stiff then fold into the batter.

Leave it for a further 10 minutes then brush a pan with oil or butter, heat and ladle the batter onto the pan in 3-inch diameter circles. (You can speed up this process by using two pans simultaneously.)

When the top of the blinis dry out and they become pitted with bubbles turn them over for a few seconds.

Drain on kitchen paper, cover with foil and keep hot in the oven. It is possible to reheat these blinis but never do so in the microwave.

Serve them with a topping of caviar, red or black lumpfish roe or smoked salmon, and a layer of sour cream.

If you wish you can flavour the sour cream with chopped chives.

On a less cosmopolitan level, our own traditional Irish breakfast can be unbeatable. Whether dished up with great simplicity at your own kitchen table or more stylishly presented at Marlfield House, where Mary Bowe has now won two best breakfast awards, there is something infinitely comforting about it. I think that we sometimes forget how superb our pork products are in this country but a long absence abroad makes one appreciate a fine platter of sausages, rashers, black and white pudding, free-range eggs and the succulent flat mushrooms that grow wild throughout the early autumn. My old Trinity contemporary Michael Bogdanov is one of the most prolific and gregarious of breakfast cooks. Theatre hours make late, relaxed breakfasts more feasible than dinners at times, and his good humour as he juggles fleets of saucepans and produces moutains of delectable food is quite intoxicating. No breakfast feast is complete for him without a generous dish of Leopold Bloom's favourite organ – the kidney. This is just one of his methods of serving it.

DEVILLED KIDNEYS BOGDANOV

8 lambs' kidneys	Skin, halve and core the kidneys.
2 oz butter	Heat the butter in a pan and brown the kidneys lightly.
1 tbsp dry mustard powder	
2 tsp Worcester sauce	Lower the heat and continue to cook very gently for about 5 minutes.
Salt and pepper to taste	Meanwhile mix the dry mustard in the Worcester sauce and add to the kidneys in the pan.

Cook gently for a few more minutes – a worthy addition to the great Irish breakfast, or delicious eaten on their own on hot, buttered toast.

The other essential component of a fine fry is, of course, soda bread, both brown and white. In compensation for hypnotising me away from nicotine, Ivor Browne used to give me the best brown bread in the world. Sadly the nicotine-free era did not last, but I still have his bread recipe.

This is a flat, unleavened bread, quite unlike the normal Irish soda bread and more like the local breads that one finds in Mediterranean countries.

BROWNE'S BREAD

3/4 lb stoneground wholemeal flour

1/4 lb plain flour

A good handful of wheat bran

A small handful of pinhead oatmeal

A good handful of vitagrain (available from health food shops)

3 or 4 tsp wheatgerm

2 tsp honey

1 tsp bread soda

1 tsp salt

1 pint buttermilk

Flaked almonds and sunflower seeds for topping

Pre-heat the oven to 400°F/Gas 6.

Mix the brown and white flour together in a large baking bowl then add the bran, oatmeal, vitagrain and wheatgerm.

Mix together well and add salt, bread soda and honey then pour in the buttermilk. Use a spoon to work the dough into a loose mix. It should be too slack to knead with the hands in the conventional way.

Cover a baking sheet with two layers of buttered silver foil and shape the dough into a flat cake shape. Use the blunt side of a knife to indent a deep cross in the dough, making four farl shapes.

Sprinkle the top of the loaf with flaked almonds and sunflower seeds. (Never put the sunflower seeds into the mix as they can discolour unattractively.)

Cook for about an hour. The bread is cooked when a knuckle tapped on the base gives a hollow sound.

Marmalade is as essential an ingredient of this sort of breakfast as tea or coffee. There are masses of smart designer marmalades on the market these days but you might like to try making your own when Seville oranges are in season.

GRAND MARNIER MARMALADE
(makes 6 1lb jars)

2 lb Seville oranges

4 pints water

1 lemon

4 lb granulated sugar

3 fl oz Grand Marnier

A 10 inch square piece of muslin (for pips and pith)

Put the water in a large pan to heat.

Cut the oranges and lemon in half, squeeze the juice out on a juicer and add it to the water in the pan.

Scoop out the pith and put it into the muslin with the pips which have been discarded after squeezing.

Tie the muslin into a firm parcel and attach with a piece of string to the handle of the pan, so that the muslin bag is floating in the water and fruit juice.

Simmer slowly, uncovered, for 2 hours then remove the muslin bag and put it on a saucer to cool down.

Warm the sugar in a bowl for about ten minutes (or until warmed through) and add to the liquid. Stir occasionally to stop crystals from forming.

Once the muslin bag has cooled down, squeeze it tightly to get all the residual liquid into the pan. (The pectin in this is an essential setting agent.)

Add the Grand Marnier and fast boil for 15-20 minutes or until the marmalade 'jells' on a cold saucer.

Warm the jam pots in the oven. Before pouring the marmalade into each pot, stand a silver spoon or fork in each one. When the marmalade is on the point of setting remove the fork or spoon, cover the jam with waxed paper discs and tie down the pots.

An excellent alternative breakfast spread is:

GINGER PRESERVE

4 lb cooking apples (windfalls are fine for this preserve)

2 pints water

2 oz root ginger, bruised and tied in a muslin bag

Sugar and preserved ginger as required (see method)

Wash and roughly chop the apples.

Do not core or peel.

Stew in the water with the muslin bag of root ginger until they are soft and pulpy then turn them into a cloth or jelly bag, suspended over a suitable container and allow the juice to drip through.

This can take some time. I often leave a jelly bag to drip overnight.

When the dripping has completely stopped measure the resulting liquid and add 1lb of sugar to each pint of juice.

Bring slowly to a rolling boil, stirring occasionally then boil quite rapidly for about 10 minutes.

When the mixture jells, add finely chopped preserved ginger to the mixture – about 4 ounces of ginger for each pound of sugar used makes a well flavoured preserve but more or less can be used according to taste.

Reboil after adding the preserved ginger and pot into jars using the method described in the previous recipe.

Although I personally never start cooking before midday I am fortunate to have good friends who do. Gill Bowler spoils one for ever after with her glorious grills and tempting mounds of muffins.

THE BOWLER BLUEBERRY MUFFIN

5 oz plain flour
½ level tsp baking powder
1 egg
1½ oz castor sugar
4 fl oz milk
2 oz butter
6 oz blueberries
½ tsp pure vanilla extract
Salt

Melt the butter and allow to cool slightly. Sieve the flour, baking powder and salt into a bowl. In another bowl mix eggs, sugar, milk, butter and vanilla extract.

Sieve the dry ingredients into the wet ones and fold in with a large spoon working as quickly as you can.

Fold the blueberries in next with as little stirring as possible. Spoon the mixture into bun cases.

Cook at 400°F/Gas 6 on a high shelf for about 30 minutes.

Years ago, when Bill and Bridgette Cussen had the Glenwood Rooms, they used to cook for their friends on Sundays when the restaurant was closed. One of their brunch dishes which will be dear to me until my dying day was...

BILL'S EGGS BERICHONNE

1 small chopped onion

4 rashers of streaky bacon, cut in thin strips

4 chopped chicken livers

2 oz butter

2 cupfuls of red wine (Pinot Noir or similar)

6 crushed peppercorns

A little powdered bouquet garni

2 tbsp chopped parsley

4 slices toast

1 clove garlic, cut in two

8 eggs

2-3 oz flour

Soften the chopped onion in the butter then add the strips of rasher and the chicken livers and cook over a gentle heat.

Set aside the onions, rashers and livers and keep warm. Then add the peppercorns, bouquet garni and flour to the pan juices, stirring well. Pour in the red wine and cook until the sauce has thickened and is slightly reduced.

Meanwhile cut roundels of toast, rub them well with the cut clove of garlic and fit them into the bottom of 8 ramekin dishes.

Top the roundels of toast with portions of the onion, rasher and liver mixture and pour a little sauce over them. Slide an egg into each ramekin. Bake the ramekins in a roasting tin containing an inch or two of hot water at 400°F/Gas 6 for 10-12 minutes.

Before serving, pour in a little more of the warm wine sauce, taking care not to cover the yolk of the egg which should remain visible in the centre of the sauce.

These brunch dishes demand a compatible wine. It's better, after all, that your guests fall flat on their faces rather than your culinary efforts. A Grand Cru is overkill but nobody will thank you for paint-stripper either. A light fruity red is ideal. I like 'Les Terrasses de Guilhelm' which makes fruity, easy drinking, especially if lightly chilled.

If brunching 'au champagne', Ayala non vintage is well worth a try and a few bottles tucked away for a year improve greatly.

If you prefer to settle for the champagne and orange juice syndrome then the Aussie Angas Brut is your only man.

My concluding recipe for this chapter might seem less breakfast and brunch oriented than the rest but I think that a brunch party can be given a pleasantly mitteleuropean flavour by something like this. Over there to the right of the E.C., breakfast feasts can include all sorts of delights which we neglect: cherry tart, sachertorte, salami sausage, mild cheese, pickled gherkins and even excellent local cognac, as I discovered on my recent trip to Prague. We shouldn't be too surprised. Fox hunting folk, here at home, scoff fruit cake and sausages washed down with port and brandy at Lawn meets and think nothing of it. Even closer to home in Europe there are those who consider fried eggs and rashers a barbarous alternative to a croissant and a bowl of coffee. So at your next brunch party try my son-in-law's cheesecake, it might go down rather well. I myself find most cheesecakes taste like wet paint but this cooked one is quite a different matter.

D AVID'S CHEESECAKE

1 packet digestive biscuits (Hob Nobs or similar)

Put the biscuits into a plastic bag and crush with a rolling pin.

2 oz butter

Melt the butter over a gentle heat and mix the crushed biscuits into it.

11 oz Philadelphia cream cheese

2 eggs

Take a greased, circular baking tin (about 8 inches diameter) and press the biscuit mixture firmly into it to create a base.

1 cup sugar

1 tsp vanilla essence

Blend the remaining ingredients in an electric blender and pour over the biscuit base.

Cook for 25-30 minutes in a moderate oven 350°F/Gas 4.

Refrigerate overnight.

Serve cold accompanied by a macédoine of fresh fruit.

Finally I would like to say that breakfast in bed, as far as I am concerned, is a non-event. Beds are for sleeping in (or not) and one thing that should be absolutely eschewed while in a semi-supine position is eating. If your loved one overrides you (so to speak) on this point make sure that he knows where the oranges, the squeezer, the coffee and the percolator are – and tell him what James Agee said: 'If music be the breakfast food of love, kindly do not disturb until lunchtime.'

Lunching with Loved Ones

*'I married the Duke for better
or worse but not for lunch.'*
Wallis Simpson.

If ever there was a sign that the romance of the century was cooling, this was it. Everyone knows that in love terms, lunch is a flirtatious assignment and dinner is the commitment. In business terms, it may be only for wimps as Gordon Gekko told us, but romantically speaking, lunch at leisure with the prospect of a long afternoon stretching ahead is pregnant with possibility, though pregnant is probably an unfortunate word to use.

There are certain rules about love lunches. If you are doing the food and he's bringing the wine, make sure everything is prepared beforehand so you don't have to get hot and bothered at the wrong moment. The only drink for such lunches is champagne and the food should be pretty and easy to eat. Finger food of an aphrodisiac nature – asparagus spears, oysters, caviar, strawberries – is ideal and idyllic. After all it should be light enough that you don't feel completely sated, not yet at any rate. A sweet and sinful pud is a provocative pause before sweet sin. The key note is sensuality. In summer be light, in winter, warming.

But of course you don't have to be in love to love lunching. Certainly some of the most memorable midday meals I've ever had didn't involve romance at all. Longest ever was with Bernardine Dewar in Locks which ended over breakfast the next day. It was fun, it was insane and some of the characters involved included Mannix Flynn, Shirley Conran, Charlie McCreevy and Ann O'Connor among others. The latter is a superlative cook and I've eaten many a fine lunch and dinner chez O'Connor. A mouth-watering example of her style is Quail Nests.

QUAIL NESTS
(serves 4)

2 dozen quails' eggs	Warm up your vol-au-vent cases in a low oven.
6 large flat mushrooms	Sauté the mushrooms in a little butter.
4 x 4 inch diameter vol-au-vent cases (bought or home-made)	When they are cooked purée them lightly in a food processor.
	Divide this purée between the pastry cases.
¾ pint Béarnaise sauce	Boil the quails' eggs for just one minute so that they are still soft in the middle then shell them carefully and put six eggs into each 'nest'.
	Warm the Béarnaise sauce and pour over the quails' eggs.

BÉARNAISE SAUCE

3 tbsp white wine or tarragon vinegar

4 oz butter

2 egg yolks

1 heaped tbsp chopped French tarragon

1 heaped tbsp chopped parsley

1 tbsp hot water

Fresh lemon juice to season

Heat the chopped tarragon and parsley in the wine or vinegar in a *bain-marie* until the volume of liquid is reduced by about two thirds.

Remove from the inner pan and whisk in the egg yolks and the hot water, then replace the pan over the simmering water in the *bain-marie* and slip in the butter in small pieces, stirring continuously.

Do not allow the sauce to boil but if it separates, remove from the heat and vigorously whisk in a little hot water. When the sauce has a thick, creamy consistency add lemon juice and a pinch of salt to taste.

Another luxurious starter or light main course is Bernardine's...

CRAB IN AUBERGINE
(6 portions, 3 main courses or 6 starters)

3 smallish aubergines

8 oz crab meat (preferably body meat)

1 onion

1 tin chopped tomatoes

4 tbsp tomato purée

1 tbsp paprika

1 tbsp chopped oregano

Cut the aubergines in half lengthways.

Brush them with oil and cook in a very low oven until the flesh is becoming tender. This should take about a quarter of an hour in a pre-heated oven (350°F/Gas 4).

Soften the onions in olive oil over a low heat then add tomatoes, paprika and purée. Continue cooking until you have a rich, thick sauce.

Season this to taste with salt and pepper then scoop out the flesh of the aubergines and add to the sauce, leaving the skin intact.

Continue to cook the sauce for a few minutes before removing from the heat and adding the crab meat and chopped oregano.

1oz grated fresh Parmesan

Pile this mixture into the aubergine shells and spread the grated cheese over the top.

1oz grated mature Cheddar

Return to the oven until the cheese has melted and begins to bubble.

Olive oil

Serve hot.

Salt and black pepper

If you wish to make this dish ahead of time or freeze it, leave the cheese topping off until the final reheat.

The best scallops since the grand old days of the Russell Hotel are to be had in Gooser's Restaurant, Killaloe, which specialises in superlative fish dishes. Roger Porrit who has practised the culinary art all over the world, gave me his special recipe.

GOOSER'S SCALLOPS
(2 main courses or 4 starters)

16 fresh scallops
¹/₄ pint cream
¹/₂ pint dry white wine
2 crushed cloves garlic
1 sprig fresh thyme
2 oz Irish white Cheddar cheese (mild Glenlara Mills or similar mild variety)
Salt and pepper
1lb creamed potato

Lightly poach the scallops in the white wine in a covered pan.

Remove the scallops and keep warm.

Add all the remaining ingredients to the liquid in the pan and reduce slowly.

When it has reached a creamy consistency sieve and return the scallops for a few minutes.

Divide the scallops and the sauce between four scallop shells and pipe creamed potato round the perimeter.

Place under a hot grill to finish and serve garnished with seaweed and a lemon wedge.

My most name-dropping lunch was in Mortons in L.A. where I started off with author Pierre Rey and his film friend Roger Vadim and ended up with author Gore Vidal and his film friend Orson Welles. I begged Orson to allow a photograph but he was down on his luck in those days doing sherry ads to keep going and wanted $500 to pose. (Even I don't charge that much.)

According to Gore Vidal, nobody is allowed to fail within a two mile radius of the Beverley Hills Hotel. I saw what he meant as I lunched the next day in the Polo Lounge with some real live Hollywood wives. The trio I lunched with were more individual than the Jackie Collins version. Micheline Connery is highly extroverted, kind-hearted and totally lovable; Joanna Poitier is gentle and warm and married to Sidney for nearly thirty years – by Hollywood standards, no mean achievement; and the stunningly beautiful Shakira, wife of Michael Caine. Lunch was diet light by my standards – cold salmon and a low calorie salad, washed down with some chilled Chablis. But this was gargantuan by L.A. standards. Most of the ladies who lunched that day around us were toying with mixed leaf salads and sipping Evian.

A mixed leaf salad is the most virtuous lunch of all but those of us who are not Hollywood wives might like to add a bit of bite to our greens. This Calpurnia salad is healthy and delicious – beyond reproach in fact.

CALPURNIA SALAD

For each person to be served you will need:

1 oz goat's cheese, cut in small cubes

1½ rashers of smoked, streaky bacon, cut in thin strips

½ slice of crustless white bread, rubbed with the cut side of a garlic clove and cut in small cubes

A level tbsp of sunflower seeds

Oil for cooking

Start this dish by making a mixed leaf salad, as colourful and fresh as possible.

Good basics are lollo rosso, radicchio, sweet rocket and iceberg lettuce with, perhaps, a few peppery leaves of dandelion, chives, watercress or nasturtium.

Once the salad leaves have been washed and dried arrange them in a bowl with plenty of room for tossing the salad later.

Fry the garlic flavoured croutons in a generous measure of hot oil and keep warm.

Fry the strips of rasher until they are crisp then keep them warm with the croutons.

Finally, crisp the sunflower seeds in the hot oil.

Toss the croutons, rasher strips and cubes of goat's cheese through the salad leaves and scatter the sunflower seeds on top.

Serve with a plain vinaigrette or blue cheese dressing.

BLUE CHEESE DRESSING

4 tbsp olive oil

1 tbsp wine vinegar

2 oz Cashel blue cheese

Salt and pepper

Beat the oil and vinegar together with salt and pepper to taste then add the cheese in small pieces and pound in well.

Mix until the consistency is even (a food processor is good for this).

Season with salt and pepper.

Irish wives are more robust, physically and mentally than their Hollywood counterparts and they'd prefer my friend Bernardine's nourishing sweetbread dish.

BOUCHÉES À LA REINE

1 pair calves' sweetbreads

8 mushrooms

6 oz ham in a thick dice

½ pint chicken stock

¼ pint cream

Juice of 1 lemon

3 oz butter

2½ oz flour

6 ready-made vol-au-vent cases

Soak the sweetbreads for about three hours, changing the water a few times, then simmer them for about 5 minutes before immersing them in fresh, cold water.

Remove all the veins and membranes, pat dry and dice.

Toss them in about 1 ounce of the butter in a warm frying pan then add the chicken stock and simmer for 15 minutes.

Slice the mushrooms and sauté them in a further 1 ounce of butter.

At this point pop the vol-au-vent cases into the oven to warm through.

Melt the remaining butter and stir in the flour to make a *roux*.

Thin this with the liquor from the sweetbreads and the cream and stir over a low heat until thick and smooth.

Add the lemon juice and season to taste then add the sweetbreads, chopped ham and mushrooms.

Simmer until warmed through and then pour into the warm vol-au-vent cases.

Mrs Melosine Bowes-Daly, a former M.F.H. of the Galway Blazers wrote a very comprehensive bi-lingual cookery book in Swahili and English in her Happy Valley days. It must have been a godsend to the Memsahibs who found the local language beyond them. This recipe, which was turned out in many an African kitchen during the 'forties was one she had obtained from London's Embassy Club before the outbreak of war. With the leaves left on the halved pineapple it is a very glamorous way to serve a chicken salad.

EMBASSY CLUB CHICKEN

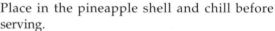

1 pineapple

1 large chicken breast

6 oz tongue, cubed

Mayonnaise

Slice the pineapple lengthways and cut out the flesh.

Remove the core and cube the remainder.

Mix this with a large cooked chicken breast, cubed, and 6 ounces of cubed tongue.

Dress this with a mayonnaise which you have made with cream in place of oil and lemon juice in place of vinegar.

Place in the pineapple shell and chill before serving.

Sunday lunch with all the family is an achievement but at least thirty times a year, we manage to get the whole crew on board ranging from my 93 year-old mother through the four generations to my three grandchildren who range in age from six down. Feeding here has to be traditional and easy enough for young and old to cope, and the second and third generations to be coaxed out of the Saturday night/Sunday morning abyss. The most important thing is to fortify yourself with a pre-prandial Bloody Mary or two.

DE MONFORD'S BLOODY MARY
(Makes 2 pints)

1 ³⁄₄ pints tomato juice

4 fl oz blue vodka

4 fl oz peach schnapps

2 tsp Worcester sauce

¹⁄₂ tsp tabasco sauce

¹⁄₂ level tsp celery salt

Freshly ground pepper

Crushed ice

2 lemons or limes, quartered

Measure the tomato juice, vodka and schnapps into a cocktail shaker or blender.

Add seasoning and mix.

Use tall glasses and quarter fill with crushed ice.

Pour mixture over ice and squeeze lemon or lime wedges into each glass and stir well.

There's no stopping the flow at that point and wine with Sunday lunch is an unbreakable tradition. However, my family, like most, includes palates which are vitiated, uneducated, undemanding, uncritical or defunct. Consequently we go for cheap and cheerful plonk which will not offend the few who can still taste it.

The wines which I include in this category are reasonably priced, decent quality Rioja style wines, such as Roblejano in either red or white. Moving up-market, but still good value there is Alsace Pinot Blanc or the white burgundy, George Faivley, Bourgogne Blanc. Failing that a Charles de France Chardonnay always goes down a treat. Another choice would be a good Sancerre, such as Vacheron.

The focal point of the feast is the roast, be it beef, lamb or pork, with all the time-honoured accompaniments and every family follows their own traditions. But Sunday is the one day when almost everybody forgets the dietary shibboleths of the week and eats a pudding. Some families maintain that there should always be a choice of at least two and that ice cream doesn't 'count'. It might, however, if you try this delicious quick sauce which Matty Ryan devised for glamourising a block of plain vanilla. Once you have made it you can keep it in a screw-top jar in the fridge for up to three weeks.

TOBLERONE SAUCE FOR ICE CREAM

1 carton cream

3 tbsp Bailey's Irish Cream Liqueur

1 oz bar Toblerone

Melt the Toblerone bar slowly in a *bain-marie* then stir in the cream and the Bailey's Irish Cream.

Use immediately or store in a jar.

This recipe is taken from an old housekeeping book of Liz Vereker's grand aunt Marion Hugill – the young chatelaine of Greenhurst in the Isle of Man who, in the 1920s, started keeping her favourite recipes. Her idea for a post-lunch pud is wonderfully intoxicating. Here it is as she wrote it down 70 years ago.

TIPSY CAKE

Take some old sponge cake and cut it into thick slices and spread them each with different jams – apricot, raspberry and marmalade.

Build them up on a glass dish with a few ratafias sprinkled among them (or some macaroons).

Then take two glasses of sherry and one of brandy mixed in a cup and a piece of sugar that has been rubbed on lemon rind and then crushed with a roller.

Mix and ladle over the cake with a spoon.

Let it stand and keep ladling the liquor over until it has absorbed it all.

Have ready some whipped cream and pile it over the cake.

Sprinkle a few ratafias over it and send to table.

Summer Pudding is a firm favourite in my family. Traditionally this dish could only be enjoyed during the short period when the seasonal ingredients were available from the kitchen garden but with the advent of the home freezer and excellent imported soft fruit it is now possible to enjoy it over a longer period

SUMMER PUDDING

2 - 2½ lb mixed strawberries, raspberries, redcurrants, loganberries and blueberries

6 oz sugar

6-8 slices of stale white bread, de-crusted

2 generous tbsp brandy

4 tbsp water

Hull and wash the fruits and soak in brandy for at least one hour: Bring the sugar and water slowly to the boil and add the fruit. Cook gently for 2-3 minutes. Do not let the fruit get soggy.

Line a buttered 2 pint pudding basin with the bread, reserving 3 slices to complete the pudding. Half fill the bowl with the fruit mixture. (This should not be too soggy or the pudding will not set properly for slicing. Drain off some of the liquid if it seems rather too moist.) Cover this fruit with another slice of bread then pour in the remainder, and make a lid from the last two slices of bread.

Put a weighted saucer on top of the completed pudding and leave in the fridge overnight. Serve with whipped cream to which you can add chopped pecans and a pinch of nutmeg if desired.

My most loved cook has to be my mother who has been cooking since Edward the Seventh was on the throne. She's not a drinker herself and doesn't know where I came from but she does lash the hooch into her Chocolate Brandy Loaf.

CHOCOLATE BRANDY LOAF

(uncooked)

½ lb digestive biscuits

½ lb Chocolat Menier *(or any bitter dark chocolate suitable for cooking)*

½ lb butter

2 eggs

3 oz vanilla sugar

2 oz glacé cherries

2 oz walnuts

1 glass brandy

Crush the biscuits coarsely. Melt the chocolate and butter in a *bain-marie*.

Beat the eggs and sugar together until they are foamy.

Combine this with the chocolate and butter mixture.

Chop the cherries and walnuts and fold into the mixture with the brandy.

Press the mixture into a greased 2 pound loaf tin and leave to set in the fridge for a minimum of four hours, preferably overnight.

When turning the loaf out, run a knife around the edges and dip the base of the tin in hot water.

Decorate it with a few more half cherries or walnuts (optional) and serve with whipped cream.

Sunday lunches are an important part of my childhood memories and even today all the family joining in the preparations beforehand (youngsters laying the table, daughters helping to cook the meal and males pouring the drinks) before sitting down together is all part of the wonderful ritual.

The Men Who Came To Dinner

'Food gives real meaning to dining-room furniture.'
Fran Lebowitz.

Let's face it. The primary reason we give dinner parties is to show off. Be it to justify the cordon bleu cookery course you've just completed at enormous expense, or to parade the hunting table you've inherited or simply to boast a celebrity guest, the dinner party is all about flaunting it.

Dinner parties should (and generally do) take lots of time, trouble and expense. But, like Nureyev dancing, it should look effortless. Put it like this: the hottest dish in the kitchen shouldn't be the hostess.

If you can keep your cool you can turn disaster into triumph. Ten years ago I was having 24 people to dinner before the ball Sir Marc Cochrane gave for his sister's 21st at Woodbrook. Everything was under control and I was swanning around dispensing largesse and large ones whereupon my housekeeper whispered in my ear that the soup was hot and ready. As this was supposed to be a sophisticated cold tomato and orange potage, I had a mild seizure and then a brainwave. I fired the contents of a large bottle of vodka into the vat and flung the lot in the freezer. Twenty minutes later my guests (a disparate collection of diplomats, divas and dingbats) sat down to drink Bloody Marys out of soup bowls. By the time we got to the main course, the joint was jumping. In thirty years of giving them, it was the best party of all.

The first rule of any dinner party is to be there for those initial sticky social moments before the food. You can't disappear into the kitchen for long intervals leaving the guests to orchestrate the mood. You must decide on a menu that doesn't need nursing: dishes that can be left in a low oven without deteriorating are ideal. Any recipe that ends with the instruction 'serve immediately' will cause chaos.

A favourite stand-by which fills these requirements is stuffed pork steak.

SUPER SWINE
(Serves 4-6)

2 large pork steaks	Split the pork steaks in two and hammer out to measure about 10" by 12".
For stuffing:	
3 slices sliced pan	Break the bread into coarse crumbs.
2 oz ham	Finely chop and cube the ham.
5 or 6 mushrooms	Dice the mushrooms.
2 eating apples	Core, peel and dice the apples and soften in butter.
4 scallions	Chop the fresh, dried herbs very finely.
1 clove garlic	Combine all these dry stuffing ingredients with the wet ones and mix well.
Fresh or dried herbs	
(Rosemary Tarragon, Basil etc.) to taste	Set aside until the liquids are absorbed then pile the stuffing onto one pork steak and cover with the other.
Salt and pepper	Using kitchen string, tie around the meat until it looks like a torpedo.

For sauce:

*½ pint medium
sherry*

Dash of lemon juice

3 fl oz cream

Awkward or mismatched corners should be secured with toothpicks to prevent the stuffing from leaking out during cooking.

Put the pork into a casserole dish with the sherry and the lemon juice and cook, tightly covered, in a slow 325°F/Gas 3 oven for about one hour.

When it is cooked, thicken the cooking liquor with the cream and hand separately as a sauce.

Carve the meat in thick slices, like a loaf of bread.

I generally precede this with a simple fish dish such as Taramasalata or smoked trout with horseradish cream and a cool fruity pudding to follow such as caramel peaches. This is a luscious dinner party pudding and has the advantage that it must be made at least four hours before eating and preferably on the preceding day.

PEACH PERFECTION

Ripe peaches, at least one per person

Ground cinnamon

Soft brown sugar

Cream to cover

Peach liqueur (2 tbsp per peach)

Blanch skin and halve enough ripe peaches to cover the base of a porcelain flan dish.

Sprinkle a few tablespoons of peach liqueur over them then dredge thickly with cinnamon.

Spread with whipped cream, making sure that its level remains below the rim of the flan dish, otherwise it will bubble up and overflow during the caramelising process.

Dredge the cream thickly with soft brown sugar and bake under a hot grill until it is caramelised.

Leave to rest for at least four hours, overnight if possible, to allow the peach juice to seep into the liqueur. If ripe peaches are not available, this dish can be made with apricots and apricot liqueur.

Serve with Amaretti, little almond macaroons.

 Serve Muscat de Beaumes de Venise with these. It's very handy as it keeps well in the fridge after opening. There are also some delicious Australian Muscats around.

I try to plan all dinner dates chez moi. If I'm frantic I call up my old pal and the best chef in the country – John Howard – and get a Coq Hardi take-away. If I'm my usual cool unflappable self I prepare Howard's End, an Oscar winning beef dish from John's kitchen.

HOWARD'S END
Rump of Beef the John Howard Way

3 lb rump beef

4 oz salt

½ oz saltpetre

4 cloves garlic

1 tsp cloves

6 juniper berries

1 bay-leaf

1 tsp chopped thyme

½ cup fresh basil

4 carrots, finely chopped

2 medium onions, finely chopped

Freshly ground black pepper

1 cup red wine

2 cups rich beef stock

Fresh parsley

Rub the meat all over with the salt and saltpetre and put it into a deep earthenware casserole dish with a tight fitting lid. Season with juniper berries, garlic cloves, bay-leaf, basil, thyme and half the carrots, one of the onions and pepper.

Cover with a cloth and then the lid.

Refrigerate and leave for one week.

Turn the meat and leave for another week.

Remove the meat from the marinade, wrap it in a cloth and put into a casserole dish with remaining carrots, onion and parsley, red wine and beef stock and cook in a low heat for three hours.

Slice and serve with puréed vegetables.

When I want to impress the dear one, I whip up a casserole of prime, young venison. Farmed deer meat is more tender and succulent than the wild variety and venison casseroles will not be ruined by tardy guests or other unforeseen delays. Jonathan and Betty Sykes, whose magnificent deer park at Springfield Castle is one of the best sights in Limerick, are constantly creating new dishes for their product. This is one of their recent creations.

THE HON. BETTY SYKES SPRINGFIELD VENISON
serves 4-6

2 lb good quality stewing venison cut into cubes

Seasoned flour

Approx. 2 oz butter

1 tbsp olive oil

6 oz finely chopped onion

2 tsp Dijon mustard

2 tsp brown sugar

Pinch of nutmeg a little ginger and allspice to taste

1 bottle of Guinness

Juice and grated rind of 2 oranges

Salt and freshly ground black pepper

Chopped parsley

Coat the venison cubes in the seasoned flour.

Melt the butter, add the oil and sauté the onions until golden over a low heat.

Increase the heat and seal the meat. Remove the venison and the onions from the frying pan and put in a casserole dish.

Pour the Guinness over the meat. I like to thin it with a little water but this is my personal taste.

Add the mustard, sugar, freshly milled black pepper, juice of two oranges and the rind of one.

At this point you can add fresh herbs to taste if you wish.

Cook until nearly tender (Betty does this in the Aga so the temperature and time can vary a little).

It should take 1 hour at 350°F/Gas 4 but check as the age of the beast can affect cooking time.

Add the remaining orange and cook for a little longer. Adjust the seasoning and serve sprinkled with a little chopped parsley.

A concoction of chestnuts complement such a rich game dish. Mary Powell who collected many of her superb recipes while doing her opera training in Italy makes this light and flavoursome charlotte.

A MOUSSE OF MARRONS

4 oz preserved chestnuts

7 fl oz milk

3 fl oz water

30 Boudoir biscuits

3 oz sugar

½ oz gelatine dissolved in 4 tbsp hot water

5 ½ oz unsweetened chestnut purée

2 tbsp orange liqueur

10 fl oz cream

Line the bottom of a mould with greaseproof paper.

Mix together 3 fluid ounces of milk and 3 fluid ounces of water.

Dip biscuits in this mixture and line the sides of the mould reserving extra biscuits for later.

If necessary, trim the biscuits to make a snug fit.

Dissolve the sugar in the remaining milk. Add the softened gelatine, the chestnut purée and the orange liqueur.

Transfer this mixture into a bowl.

Chill this mixture until it begins to set (30 minutes or more).

Drain and chop the whole preserved chestnuts. Beat the cream until thick but not stiff.

Beat half of this cream into the gelatine mixture then fold in the rest with the chopped chestnuts.

Spoon all of this into the mould and fit the leftover Boudoir biscuits on top.

Cover with greaseproof paper and chill overnight before turning out.

This recipe gives generous helpings for six people and freezes beautifully.

Of course dinner parties do not sustain themselves on food alone. Conversation and compatibility are just as important as the cuisine. Always put as wide a distance as possible between males who are keen on rugby or golf. It is so sad to see amusing women of artistic but indolent taste glazing over as the latest game is replayed in detail across them. Some hostesses actually plan a few controversial openings in advance to retrieve these situations and bring the talk back into more general channels.

Elspeth Huxley, as a young girl, was advised by an Irish cousin how to deal with such eventualities: 'Think out in advance a couple of openings and cast them like flies upon the water. One that I have found useful is; "I understand persimmons are in season. Served with peacocks' tongues and stewed in Bactrian honey they are more appetising, don't you think , than pomegranates with all those tiresome seeds?" ...I have never known it to fail.'

I have never, fortunately, been reduced to enlivening a mute party with this gambit but I fear that it would hardly engender riotous debate amongst my own intimates. However, pomegranates are very good with fowl and game if you can get rid of all those 'tiresome seeds' as the following dish will demonstrate. You can prepare the sauce ahead of time so it fits into my minimum fuss philosophy and makes a delightful dish for a cosy quartet.

PHEASANT OR DUCK WITH
POMEGRANATE SAUCE

1 large duck or a brace of pheasant

2 oz butter

1 finely chopped onion

6 oz ground walnuts

½ pint pomegranate juice (squeezed on a manual, not electric squeezer. The vigour of an electric extractor can crush the pith and make the juice bitter).

1 tsp sugar

3 or 4 tbsp fresh lime juice

Take the neck and giblets of a large duck or a brace of pheasant and simmer for about 40 minutes to make a stock.

Do not include the bird liver in this dish. Set it aside for some other purpose.

Roast the birds in the usual way with an onion in the body cavity until cooked. Meanwhile prepare the sauce.

Fry the onion in butter and remove the pan from the stove in order to add the ground walnuts.

Pour in the pomegranate juice, strained giblet stock, sugar and lime juice.

Cover and simmer very slowly for half an hour.

When the duck or pheasant is cooked add to this sauce the juices from the roasting pan and the essences which drain from the body cavity of the birds.

Garnish the birds with whole pomegranate seeds, slices of lime and half walnuts. Serve the sauce as an accompaniment. I like to drink a light red Burgundy such as Rully with this.

Flesh and fowl are not the only options for a dinner, Fish is delish too. Pat Moore of the Beginish restaurant in Dingle always cooks me this sea trout in saffron sauce. The proof is in the eating.

Beginish Beguilement

8 sea trout fillets, 7-8 oz each

4 fl oz dry white wine

2 finely chopped shallots

4 fl oz whipped cream

2-3 oz cold cubed butter

Extra knobs of butter to put on top of the fish while cooking

A few strands of saffron

Seasoning to taste

Optional, for garnish – blanched mangetout cut into julienne strands or some sprigs of chervil

Cut each fillet in half diagonally.

Place white wine, chopped shallots, saffron strands and fish into a baking dish.

Place half of the cut fillets skin side up and half skin side down in the dish.

Dot tops of fish with knobs of butter. Cover with tinfoil and bake in the oven at 400°F/Gas 6 for 7 to 8 minutes (careful not to overcook).

When cooked, remove the fish from the baking dish and use the liquid as a base for the sauce which is made on top of the stove.

Reduce this sauce if necessary (that is, if you have been too open handed with your wine) and add the whipped cream before whisking in the cold, cubed butter. Season to taste.

Put the sauce on the plate first with the fish on top of it.

Each portion should have one piece of fish skin side up and one piece of skin side down.

Garnish with a julienne of mangetout or a sprig of chervil.

Serve with steamed potatoes and a green vegetable.

Try a Menetou Salun from the Loire with this.

If I were to suggest my perfect dinner party for both the palate and the eye, the menu would start with a perfect mousse of shellfish followed by an unusual roast and a pudding which is neither hot nor cold. The mousse of crab and prawn is another of Mary Powell's specials.

MOLLUSC MOUSSE

1 lb white crab meat
½ pint velouté sauce (1 oz butter, 1 oz flour, ½ pint chicken stock)
½ oz gelatine
2½ fl oz white wine
½ pint mayonnaise
¼ pint whipped cream
½ lb cooked and shelled prawns

Garnish
4 tbsp French dressing
½ tsp paprika pepper/tabasco
1 peeled cucumber

Oil a dish or tin. Prepare the velouté sauce (melt the butter, stir in the flour and slowly add the stock over a low heat, stirring until thickened) and allow to cool.

Soak the gelatine in wine and allow to dissolve over a low heat.

Add it to the velouté sauce with the mayonnaise.

Fold in the crab meat and the cream. Finally add the prawns.

Put it into the oiled dish and leave it to set.

When it is set, which will take at least three hours, turn the mousse out.

In the meantime, cut the peeled cucumber into thin slices and flavour them with French dressing, paprika and tabasco sauce.

Arrange these around the mousse as a garnish.

A most baronial and glamorous main course for a political party of about ten is a whole suckling pig. This dish was inspired by politician Michael McDowell who was given a present of a pulchritudinous pig which he duly named Terry. The pig proved too intelligent for the McDowell ménage and had to leave. I am particularly fond therefore of:

MUC ROSTAITHE McDOWELL

1 suckling pig of about 3 weeks old (approx, 10 lb weight)

10 fl oz brown rum

10 fl oz olive oil

2 level tbsp salt

Fresh thyme, sage and bay-leaves

10 fl oz honey

Enough butter muslin to wrap the suckling pig

5 or 6 oz ground cloves

Truss the prepared piglet.

If your oven space allows, truss it with the legs outstretched. Otherwise fold them underneath the belly. Insert a wooden plug in the mouth and wrap the tail and ears in foil to prevent them from singeing.

Rub salt into the skin.

Baste the piglet with the honey and cloves mixed together and cover with herbs. Wrap it in the muslin and place on a rack in a large roasting tin.

Cook it on the lower shelf of a pre-heated oven (325°F /Gas 3).

Allow about 25 minutes to each pound weight.

Baste every 15 minutes with mixed rum and oil plus any of the honey and clove mixture which might have run into the pan from the cooking.

When the cooking is finished unwrap the ears and tail and remove the wooden plug from the mouth.

Replace this with a large rosy apple.

To carve, cut off its head and forelegs and the rear portion of the hind legs.

Slit along and through the backbone.

Remove the flesh from the ribcage and carve the meat and crackling into narrow strips.

Carve the shoulder and legs in wider slices.

Recommended wine with this would be a Jurancon sec.

After a main course like this, the carver, at least, will welcome something cool and simple like this ice-cream dish.

HOT AND COLD ICE-CREAM

Melted butter

8 scoops of vanilla ice-cream

16 sheets of filo pastry

Filo pastry can be bought frozen in supermarkets and has a million uses. The important thing is not to let it dry out while working with it. Keep it covered with a little film and a damp cloth to prevent it from becoming brittle.

Take one scoop of vanilla ice-cream for each person (eight in this case). Put the scoops of ice-cream, separated, onto a tray and freeze until rock hard.

For each scoop of ice-cream take two full sheets of filo pastry. Spread out the first sheet and brush all over with melted butter then lay the second sheet on top of it.

Fold the two sheets in half making four layers in all of filo. Wrap the hard frozen portions of ice-cream in the pastry, making sure that there is a good seal (use a pastry brush dipped in water for this).

Deep fry the parcels at 375°F/Gas 5 until the pastry is just golden and crispy. This should not take longer than three minutes. Sift with castor sugar.

Food of course is only a component of the mosaic that makes a dynamic dinner party. But if the food is right, then the hostess is happy and the latter, not the former, is the real secret to superlative entertaining.

Supping with the Devil & Other Attractive Folk

'... the ordinary late dinner of the upper and upper middle class, and the more unpretentious 'high tea' now so often served in small households, renders a guest or family supper a rarely seen repast.'
Mrs Beeton.

For once the redoubtable Mrs B. got it wrong. Supper parties survived and remain one of the most convivial forms of entertainment. The fact that they usually follow some other entertainment – a theatre, concert or cocktail party – means that guests arrive in good form and more than ready to sing for the food that awaits. The informality of feasting without fuss has a particular appeal for me.

During the 'eighties there was a vogue for kitchen suppers, possibly because kitchens, at that stage, were becoming 'designed' rather than starkly functional. They usually took place after cocktail parties, such as one of Maureen Cairnduff's monthly 'First Fridays', to which she would invite any smart strangers who happened to be in town as well as the regular hard core. Sometimes a group of us would repair to Bernardo's in Lincoln Place. Otherwise we would go on to somebody's house, frequently mine.

Simplicity was the keynote. After all those cocktails we went straight into a main course and wine with no first course. The dishes were unpretentious and hearty, usually based on mince – lasagne, spaghetti bolognese, chilli con carne, curried koftas – or a chicken stir fry, all of which could be prepared well in advance and could stretch to accommodate elastic guest lists. Vast green salads, garlic bread and groaning cheese boards provided the soakage necessary to keep us carousing late into the night. As happens, some hostesses became competitive and the casual suppers evolved into four course dinners, completely departing from the original pattern.

Curry is an ideal supper dish and the undisputed maestro of the curry pot for our generation was Gerald Hanley. The years that he spent in India, which gave birth to so many of his fine novels, also left him with an extensive repertoire of Indian dishes. Some like it hot – but others don't and if your taste is for a milder curry you could cut down on the quantities of chillies in this recipe.

GERALD HANLEY'S CURRY SUPPER
(Serves 4)

4 chicken breast fillets

4 onions, finely chopped

5 small, hot, green chillies

1 inch fresh ginger

2 cloves garlic, chopped

1 can chopped tomatoes

3 cloves, ground

2 cardamons, ground

3 tbsp ground coriander

1½ tbsp ground cumin

1½ tbsp turmeric

4 large potatoes, cut into chunks

1 handful of finely chopped fresh coriander leaves

Oil for cooking

Heat ½ inch of oil in a heavy bottomed pan.

Chop the chillies and the ginger finely and start to cook them very slowly in the oil. Add the two cloves of garlic.

When this mixture has softened add the tomatoes, breaking them up well. Add the ground cloves and cardamons.

If the mixture looks too dry you can add a little hot water at this stage, or at any later stage when you might feel that the consistency is becoming too thick.

Spread the sliced onions above this simmering liquid in the pot and then sprinkle the ground coriander and the cumin over them.

Cook this as slowly as possible until the oils begin to emerge and then sprinkle on the turmeric. (Remember that turmeric burns very easily.)

Cook the mixture at the lowest possible simmer for 10 minutes then add the chicken breasts and, finally, the potatoes.

Cook for at least another half hour. Add the fresh coriander and stir through well about 10 minutes before serving.

Note: Never rush a curry. Remember that the slower and longer the cooking process the better the flavour.

A lemon pickle is a great complement to any curried chicken dish and here are two of Gerry's authentic Indian recipes for this citrus relish.

GERRY'S MINCED LEMON PICKLE

2 lb lemons

1 lb seeded raisins

2 tsp ground ginger

1 oz garlic cloves

1 tsp chilli powder

1½ pints vinegar

1½ lb moist brown sugar

1 lb coarse salt

Cut the lemons in four. Remove the pips and soak with the salt in a bowl for four days, stirring often.

On the third day peel the garlic cloves and put them to soak for 24 hours in a little of the vinegar with the raisins, chilli and ginger.

On the fourth day take the lemons out of the salt and put them through a mincer with the raisin mixture.

Put the rest of the vinegar in a saucepan and add the sugar.

Mix well and add the lemon and raisin mince.

Bring to the boil then simmer very slowly until the liquid has reduced and thickened.

Let it get quite cold then bottle in sterilised jars.

This pickle can be eaten after four days but improves continually with time.

GERRY'S SALT LEMON PICKLE

1 lb lemons

4 oz green ginger

4 oz fresh green chillies

1¼ lb rock salt

4 oz chilli powder

Wash and dry the lemons.

Scrape the ginger, wash, dry thoroughly and slice into thin slivers. Wash and dry the chillies and slice in half lengthways.

Put the salt and chilli powder into a bowl and mix together. Make a cross shaped incision on each lemon, running a sharp knife crossways and then lengthways but making sure that you keep the lemon intact.

Put the lemons in the bowl and stuff with the salt mixture through the cross-shaped aperture that you have made.

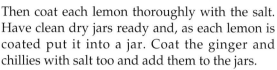

Then coat each lemon thoroughly with the salt. Have clean dry jars ready and, as each lemon is coated put it into a jar. Coat the ginger and chillies with salt too and add them to the jars.

Top up each jar with salt mixture before sealing. In India the jars are then stood in the hot sun for 2 or 3 weeks.(!)

The Irish solution is to give the jars 24 hours in a low oven. The warming oven of an Aga would be ideal. Failing that use 250°F/Gas ½.

This pickle will be ready to eat in about two month's time.

Whether the devil is coming to supper or not, one dish you will certainly need a long spoon (or fork) for is a fondue. Most of us have a fondue set gathering dust somewhere in our cupboards. On a winter evening in a cosy kitchen this forgotten dish conjures up a jolly après ski sort of atmosphere. It does turn into a bit of a scrum with more than six people so plan it for an evening when you are not going to be overrun by unexpected extras. Just to remind you of what we all used to enjoy so much, here are a few classic recipes.

THREE CHEESE FONDUE
(serves 4 -6)

1 garlic clove, halved

½ pint dry white wine

1 tsp cornflour

4 tbsp Kirsch

8 oz Gruyère or Emmenthal cheese

8 oz Beaufort or Danbo cheese

8 oz Comté cheese

Black pepper

9 - 12 slices of day old bread cut into cubes

Rub the clove of garlic firmly round the inside of a flameproof casserole.

Put the cheeses and the wine into the casserole and stir over a moderate heat until the cheeses have all melted. Grind in plenty of pepper.

Stir the kirsch and the cornflour together to make a paste and add to the casserole and stir until you have an even, creamy texture. Bring it up to a boil and transfer, still bubbling, to the spirit lamp.

The fondue will continue to cook as people dip their bread in and the mixture will get thicker as the quantity goes down.

Add a little wine, or more Kirsch.

The thin crust or *bonne bouche* which will have formed on the bottom of the dish is delicious.

Share it around and pour out the Gewurztraminer.

BEEF FONDUE FOR 6

3 lb of tender fillet of beef cut into cubes

2 or 3 cups of walnut oil

1 tbsp peppercorns

½ clove of garlic

Heat the oil in a flame proof pan until bubbling then transfer carefully to the spirit lamp. Add the crushed peppercorns and the crushed garlic.

One of the nice things about beef fondue is that people can dip their cubes of fat into the hot meat for as long as they like, so it is one of the rare occasions when the blue beef fiend and the charcoal black fanatic are both perfectly satisfied.

Lots of people prefer beer with this but I like a Chianti Classico.

Two excellent dips for the cooked cubes of beef are:

DO-GONG DIP

3 hard boiled eggs

½ tsp Dijon mustard

½ tsp English mustard

Salt

8 fl oz olive oil

4 tbsp vinegar

1 crushed clove garlic

2 gherkins, chopped

1 tsp each of tarragon, chervil, chopped chives

2 tsp parsley

10 capers, chopped

Peel the hard boiled eggs, cut in half and separate the whites from the yolks.

Cut the whites into strips and set aside. Mash the yolks on a bowl and add mustards and salt and mix well.

Drip the oil in slowly, whisking all the time.

As the mixture begins to thicken you can gradually increase the flow of oil and start adding the vinegar.

The sauce should have a velvety consistency, between cream and mayonnaise.

Finish by stirring the garlic, herbs, sliced egg-white, capers and gherkins through the sauce.

DUBOIS DIP

1 onion

1 cup dry white wine

1 cup soured cream

2 tbsp lemon juice

1 tsp plain flour

2 tbsp butter

Salt and pepper

Melt the butter slowly in a small, heavy based saucepan.

Slice and sauté the onion.

Add the wine and bring to the boil until it is reduced by about half.

Combine flour and soured cream and add it, a little at a time, to the hot liquid, stirring continuously.

Bring back to the boil and then strain through a fine sieve.

Discard the onion and flavour the sauce with lemon juice, salt and pepper.

Keep warm on a hot plate while it is being used for a dip.

Hearty soup can be comforting in the small hours. A muscular minestrone, mulligatawny or *gulyas* soup followed by a cheese board and crusty bread makes a fine kitchen supper. Paul Lynam first knocked up this chowder at his summer house in Kilkee, using locally available ingredients.

PAUL LYNAM'S KILKEE CHOWDER

2 lb mussels (in shells)

1 lb cockles

1 tbsp chopped parsley or chervil

6 fl oz dry white wine

8 oz potatoes cut in ¼ inch cubes

4 oz finely chopped onions

4 oz boiled belly bacon, cut in ¼ inch cubes

1½ oz butter (unsalted)

1 tbsp chopped chives

4 fl oz cream

Black pepper

Clean the mussels, discarding any that are open.

Put them in a pan with the white wine and the parsley or chervil, cover and cook over a high heat until the shells open.

Drain the liquid from the pan and retain it for stock.

When the mussels have cooled a little take them out of their shells.

Meanwhile, in a separate pan cook the cockles, covered in water.

When the cockles are open discard the water, take the cockles out of their shells and set aside with the mussels.

Cook the diced onion in butter, covered, over a medium heat for about 4 minutes.

Add diced bacon and diced potatoes and continue to cook, covered, for a further 4 minutes, stirring occasionally.

Add cockles, mussels and the cooking liquid from the cockles, bring to a boil and stir in chopped chives and cream.

Midnight feasting can, for some, be a prelude to a night of ghastly indigestion. If you want to play it safe with potentially bilious guests you can't go far wrong with simple chicken or turkey dishes. John Howard of the Coq Hardi gave me this wholesome recipe for Coq au vin.

COQ AU VIN COQ HARDI

1 large chicken jointed into 8 pieces

½ lb streaky bacon

½ lb tiny shallots

2 tbsp Cognac

1 bottle red Burgundy

1 cup veal stock

2 whole cloves garlic

1 bouquet garni, sprig of thyme, bay-leaf and parsley tied together in a muslin bag

1 lb mixed mushrooms

4 tbsp butter

Beurre manié

Salt and black pepper

Cut the bacon into lardons and blanch. Fry the pieces in butter in a heavy casserole dish.

Sauté the chicken and the onions until they are lightly coloured.

Warm the Cognac and flame the bird. Add wine, stock, garlic and bouquet garni then bring to a simmer.

Cover the casserole and cook very slowly until the chicken is tender and cooked through.

Remove the garlic cloves and the bouquet garni and add the shallots.

Cook the mushrooms in butter and slip them into the casserole dish.

Add enough small pieces of *beurre manié* (equal quantities of butter and flour) to thicken the sauce to a rich, creamy consistency.

Cook gently for another ten minutes and adjust the seasoning before serving.

John also likes to do this dish with a puff pastry lid as an interesting variation.

There are times when I know that I am going to be too smashed to go near the kitchen and that the horde of revellers I will inevitably invite back will be too smashed to pretend, politely, that they are not ravenous. When I am going to a potentially riotous drinks party I put this elegant buffet dish in the fridge. Simona Caccialupi often prepares this turkey buffet for her guests in Rome. It is a superb supper on a summer evening.

SIMONA CACCIALUPI'S TURKEY BUFFET
(serves 8)

1 whole turkey breast on the bone

5 oz capers

4 oz parsley

1 glass dry white wine

Wine vinegar

Best olive oil

Salt and pepper

Put the turkey in a roasting tin with salt and pepper, $\frac{1}{2}$ glass of olive oil and 1 glass of white wine. Cover with foil and cook in a very moderate oven (300°F -350°F) until it is cooked.

The time will obviously vary slightly depending on the size of the turkey.

Meanwhile prepare the sauce by putting 4 ounces of capers, 4 ounces of parsley, 3 tablespoons of wine vinegar, 6 tablespoons of olive oil and 2 tablespoons of cold water into a blender and liquidising.

When the turkey is cooked allow it to get quite cold then carve into thin slices and arrange on a large serving dish, brushing each slice with a good layer of the sauce and a few additional capers.

Chill for at least two hours before serving.

If visitors come from out of State it is always interesting for them to sample our traditional national dishes. Nothing could be more down-home local than bacon and cabbage. John F. Kennedy was given it at his State banquet up in the Park and raved about it. When well cooked it can compete with any other national dish in the world. The best ham and cabbage I have ever tasted is my pal Julie Campbell's which she calls, with every justification, Poet's Pig. She gets all her hams free range from Seamus Hogan of Kanturk. Whether it is the Hogan magic or the Campbell charisma, or a combination of both, I have simply never had it so good.

THE HOGAN/CAMPBELL POET'S PIG

Ham of desired size and cut

1 whole carrot, peeled

1 whole onion, peeled

1 whole stick of celery

1 cup of dry cider

6 cloves

3 bay-leaves

Mustard powder

Demerara sugar

Make sure that your ham pan is sufficiently large to leave the entire piece of meat completely immersed in water overnight. In the morning pour out the water and replace with fresh cold water.

Put the pan on the stove and bring it to the boil very slowly. If the water gets foamy as it comes to the boil this means that the bacon is still quite salty so discard it and replace with fresh water after it has been kept at a rolling boil for about ten minutes.

At this point, when you have changed the water again if necessary, add all the other ingredients except the mustard and sugar. Simmer it for about half an hour without a lid then cover the ham pot tightly and transfer to a pre-heated low oven (about 300°F - 350°F/Gas 2-3).

Cooking time depends on the weight. Allow half an hour per pound, plus one hour over.

When it is cooked remove from the pot and slice off all the skin but leave a good layer of fat behind.

Score the fat in a criss cross pattern with a sharp knife. Mix together an appropriate quantity of powdered mustard and Demarara sugar and, using your hands spread it evenly all over the fat. Put the meat in a roasting tin, protecting any exposed meat around the sides with tinfoil leaving the glazed fat exposed. Put it in a hot oven (425°F/Gas 7) until the glaze is crisp and golden brown.

Accompany with: Beautifully boiled potatoes which have been cooked with a few sprigs of fresh mint and tossed in a generous amount of butter and chopped parsley before serving.

The freshest cabbage you can get with the stalk removed and the leaves finely shredded. Stir-fry it in a frying pan with 3 tablespoons of olive oil and $1/2$ teaspoon of sesame oil. When it starts to sizzle, sprinkle on a teaspoon of caraway seeds and cover the pan. Make sure that it does not burn and serve it while it is still crunchy.

PERFECT PARSLEY SAUCE

$1^{1}/_{2}$ oz flour

$1^{1}/_{2}$ oz butter

$1/2$ pint milk

4 tbsp finely chopped parsley

Melt the butter over a low heat and stir in the flour to make a paste *(roux)*.

Mix thoroughly and add the milk gradually, stirring continuously until the sauce thickens. Do not allow it to boil.

Add the parsley to the thickened sauce and leave it for a while to allow the flavour to infuse.

Re-heat gently before serving.

Julie favours a good, fairly mature Châteauneuf du Pape. The best has to be Château Beaucastel which is quite marvelous. A good, inexpensive choice in the Châteauneuf style is Val Joanis.

My daughter, Jane, who has a vocational passion for cooking has devised this cheap and cheerful chilli dish for evenings when she has a gang of friends around. She serves it with green salads and masses of cold beer and I've christened it...

JANE'S FOUR-WAY CHILLI
(serves 12)

3 onions

3 cloves garlic

2 tins baked beans

2 tins kidney beans

2 tins chopped tomatoes

4 tbsp chilli powder

1 tube tomato purée

Paprika to taste

2 or 3 tbsp cooking oil

4½ lb minced beef

½ lb blue cheese

4 tbsp mayonnaise

A dash of milk

Chop the onions and garlic and sweat in a little cooking oil.

Add the mince and gently brown, stirring frequently.

Add the tomatoes, the purée, the chilli and continue to cook for another ten minutes.

Finally add the baked beans and the kidney beans and season to taste with paprika.

Serve the chilli on a bed of rice and offer an optional garnish of finely chopped raw onion and the blue cheese sauce, which is made by mashing the cheese and adding mayonnaise and milk together until it has the consistency of thick cream.

When Jane cooks this for my pals I give them a robust red wine such as Roblejano or a fruity white such as dry Muscat Blanc. (Brown Brothers of Australia have a nice one.)

Jane's sister, Madeleine, is not so keen on the kitchen but she can be prevailed upon, occasionally, to whip up her rice supper for family and friends. It is so delicious that, for years, none of us would believe that she had made it herself.

MADELEINE'S RISOTTO IN A RUSH

2 onions

1 can tomatoes

1 small packet frozen sliced French beans

1 small packet frozen peas

1 small can sweet corn

2 chicken breast fillets

4 eggs

2 cups of rice

1 red pepper

Soy sauce, salt and pepper for seasoning

Put the rice on to cook and whisk up the eggs with salt and pepper to taste.

Make an omelette and roll it up like a pancake.

Keep it warm while you chop and sauté the onion and the chicken, which you have cut into bite-size pieces.

Cook the beans in boiling water and drain. Then add, with the tomatoes and the sweet corn, to the onions and chicken.

When the rice is cooked drain it and throw it into a very hot, oiled wok with the other ingredients.

Add 2 teaspoons of soy sauce and other seasonings to taste.

Cut the warm omelette into thin strips and use as a garnishing layer on top of the rice.

Madeleine's quick cook ups are normally just mid-week, impromptu family affairs. None of us want morning-after blues as a result of these convivial evenings so we stick to something safe such as Blanc de Brau, an organic wine, similar to Muscadet, as the fewer the chemicals the smaller the hangover. As I always say, the family that revives together thrives together.

No late-night binge is complete without a little something to indulge the sweet toothed. Good resolutions about eschewing puddings (and other things too) tend to waver after midnight. This Russian Easter pudding is a feast fit for a Tsar. It requires no cooking and is a handy thing to produce from the fridge when calorie counting chums fall off the wagon.

PASKVA

³/₄ lb curd cheese (cream cheese will do at a pinch)

Mix the cheese and yoghurt thoroughly together with the sugar.

4 oz ground almonds

Chop all the fruit and nuts and fold them into the cheese mixture with the sieved ground almonds.

4 oz glacé cherries

2 oz dried apricots

Press this mixture down into a very well oiled pudding bowl and chill for at least four hours before turning out.

2 oz walnuts or hazelnuts

Garnish it with a few halved cherries and finely chopped nuts.

1 pot of natural yoghurt

1 tbsp castor sugar

The key to supper is of course simplicity. Don't deviate from this: if guests are invited for a relaxed meal around the kitchen table, they want to lounge over linguini not linger over langoustine.

Tippling into Temptation

'Alcohol is like love: the first kiss is magic, the second is intimate, the third is routine. After that you just take the girl's clothes off.'
Raymond Chandler, The Long Good-bye.

When asked whether he knew that drinking was a slow death, the American humorist Robert Benchley replied, 'So who's in a hurry?' Who indeed? Drink is one of the great pleasures of life and one with which I am very familiar: after all, eat, drink and remarry is one of my personal codes. But the one way I don't want to take my drink is on the drip, at one of mankind's worst inventions, the cocktail party.

Bitter experience has taught me that no one will thank you for an invitation to drinks; guests will inevitably harbour dark suspicions that their hostess is merely discharging the drearier obligations of her 'B' list (people she owes but can't be bothered to talk to) by cramming them into a smokey crush where they cannot sit down and do not get fed.

Generosity is the key and never giving wine-only parties has been a lifelong philosophy. No dedicated drinker wants to change their clothes and drive for miles to be greeted with the most depressing question in the English language, "Red or white?" It can get even worse.

There was one memorable Lenten entertainment where I was offered a choice of Rhubarb or Elderberry and, of course, there is always cup, those chunks of greengrocery floating in dubious liquid. Almost anything in a bottle can be put into a wine cup but one ingredient always present in great abundance is water. Chesterton sums up my feelings about cups perfectly: 'As Noah often said to his wife when they sat down to dine: "I don't care where the water goes if it doesn't get into the wine."'

A well stocked bar, the space to get at it and plenty of blotting paper is my formula. Once this is provided it is essential to keep plenty of food in circulation. Sausages are always popular. They may lack originality but there is never one left however many I cook. They are equally good on their own or in a honey and mustard glaze but Joan Collins, like myself, hates drippy eats down her designer duds. She serves these sausages at her drinks parties.

SOAP QUEEN'S SAUSAGES

60 cold, grilled
cocktail sausages

$7\frac{1}{2}$ oz cream
cheese
(Philadelphia)

4 tsp Mango
chutney

$3\frac{1}{2}$ oz toasted
almonds, finely
ground

Make sure the sausages are completely cold.

Slice lengthways down the centre.

Mix the cream cheese and Mango chutney.

Put this mixture into the slit in the sausages, being careful not to break them in half.

Sprinkle the toasted ground almonds over the cream cheese filling and serve.

Sesame toasts and mini quiches can be prepared in advance and warmed over when needed. They are both irresistible.

SESAME TOASTS

8 oz peeled cooked
prawns

2 tbsp cornflour

1 tbsp dry sherry

4 tbsp sesame
seeds

1 pinch salt

1 lightly beaten egg

Crustless white
sliced bread
(4-6 slices
depending on size)

Oil for frying

Pound the prawns, egg, sherry, cornflour and salt to make paste.

Spread this on one side of the sliced bread and dip the bread, prawn-side down into the sesame seeds.

Fry in fairly deep hot oil for about one minute.

Cut each slice into small rectangles before serving.

Mini Quiches of Artichoke Hearts and Mozzarella

(2 dozen mini quiches)

For pastry:

8 oz plain flour

2 oz lard

2 oz firm margarine

2 tbsp water

Pinch of salt

Rub the fats into the flour and salt until the mixture is like fine breadcrumbs.

Mix to a firm dough with the water and knead well.

Roll out thinly, cut into rounds and fit into greased patty tins.

For filling:

½ pint of mixed milk and cream (50/50)

3 eggs

1 tin artichoke hearts, roughly chopped

8 oz Mozzarella cheese

Grated Parmesan

Beat the eggs. Heat the milk and cream mix until nearly boiling then stir in the eggs.

Put a piece of artichoke heart into each patty case, pour a little of the milk cream and egg mixture over it and top with a thin slice of Mozzarella cheese and a sprinkle of Parmesan.

Bake at about 400°F/Gas 6 for 15-20 minutes.

The crab quiche filling given in *Life is a Picnic* p.89, is also ideal for filling small individual pastry shells.

Something hot and cheesy is always appetising. My party animals devour these petites *gougères*.

GOUGÈRES

3 oz butter

5 oz sifted flour

3 eggs

2½ oz Gruyère cheese

Pinch of salt

Milk for brushing

Put the butter and salt into a saucepan with half a pint of water and bring to a boil.

Remove from the heat and add the flour. Stir well.

Return to a very gentle heat and continue stirring until the mixture forms a ball.

Take off the heat again and beat in the eggs, one at a time. (A food processor is very useful for this.)

Grate the cheese and add to the dough.

Use a teaspoon to make small mounds of the mixture on a well-oiled baking sheet.

Glaze each little *gougère* with milk.

Bake at 400°F/Gas 6 for 10-12 minutes and serve warm.

One of my happiest memories of Spanish holidays are the delicious *tapas* which are always served with a drink in even the most modest *tavernas*. Nibbles with the flavours of the Mediterranean can brighten up a drinks party even on the chilliest of winter evenings. Here are three of my favourite holiday souvenirs.

HUEVOS RELLENOS
(stuffed eggs)

6 bantam eggs or the smallest hens' eggs available

4 oz tuna fish

2 tbsp mayonnaise

1 clove garlic, crushed

6 capers, chopped

Paprika for garnish

Hard boil the eggs.

When they are cold halve them lengthways and scoop out the yolks.

Pound the yolks with the other ingredients to make a paste.

Season with salt and pepper and pile the mixture back into the egg whites.

Sprinkle with paprika and serve.

PISSALADIÈRE

1 packet frozen shortcrust pastry

4-5 onions

2 cloves garlic

2 large beef tomatoes

1 tin anchovies

A handful of black olives halved and pitted

Olive oil for cooking

Roll out the pastry and line a quiche tin, not a china or porcelain one. If you want the base very crispy you can bake this blind but it is not necessary.

For the filling, slice the onions and sweat them slowly in olive oil with the two cloves of garlic finely crushed until they are thoroughly cooked but not coloured. Skin and chop the tomatoes and add them to the onions. Cook very slowly for a further ten minutes.

Pour this mixture onto the pastry base. Slice the anchovies into thin strips and use them to make a lattice pattern across the top of the onion mixture. Place a halved, pitted black olive in each rectangular space made by the lattice of anchovies. Bake at 400°F/Gas 6 for roughly 25 minutes.

TORTILLA

2 large potatoes, cut in ¹/₂ inch cubes

Put cubed potatoes, sliced onions and crushed garlic into a large frying pan where you have pre-heated a few tablespoons of olive oil.

2 medium sized onions

2 cloves garlic

4 back rashers

Cook very slowly with the lid on, stirring occasionally until the potatoes are *al dente*. In the meantime, cook the French beans and chop them into ¹/₄ inch pieces and grill the rashers and chop them coarsely.

¹/₂ cup frozen French beans

Slice mushrooms finely and add to the potatoes, onions and garlic to the frying pan.

4-6 mushrooms

8 eggs

Cook until they are soft. Beat the eggs well and season with salt and pepper.

Olive oil for cooking

Any fresh herbs (optional)

Scatter the french beans, rashers and any herbs you have over the potato mixture then pour the beaten eggs over the contents of the frying pan and cook slowly for about 15 minutes until the egg has set.

Take a suitably sized plate and invert it over the frying pan.

Holding it firmly, turn over the pan continuing to hold the plate over it and turn the omelette onto the plate.

Spread the frying pan with fresh olive oil and slide the omelette back to brown the other side.

This *tortilla* can be eaten hot to cold. When serving it as *tapas* at a cocktail party cut it into cubes and serve with a small container of toothpicks.

If you have foreign visitors at your drinks party they are equally taken by our own smoked Irish salmon which we all take for granted. There are many delicious ways of serving this, not least thinly sliced on our own brown soda bread with fresh lemon slices. Joan (Collins) has two sophisticated recipes for this versatile fish.

CRISPY SALMON PURSES

(2 dozen)

1 packet of filo pastry

1/2 lb smoked salmon

4 oz Boursin

Oil for brushing the filo pastry

Defrost the pastry and as you use each sheet keep the remaining sheets covered with cling film and a moist J-cloth to prevent them from drying out.

Spread out one sheet of pastry, brush it with oil and cover with a second sheet.

Brush that too with oil. Now slice the double layer of pastry into 3 or 4 strips lengthways (the narrower the strips the neater fingered you will need to be in folding them).

Put a small chunk of smoked salmon and a coffee spoonful of Boursin onto the base of each strip.

Fold them up in a triangular shape like small samosas. (There is an illustration of this technique in most packets of commercial filo pastry.)

Bake in a pre-heated oven, about 400°F/Gas 6 for about 12-15 minutes.

SMOKED SALMON ST. TROPEZ

*8 oz shortcrust
pastry*

*8 oz smoked
salmon, sliced
thinly*

8-10 quails' eggs

Lemon mayonnaise

*Fresh lemon cut in
wafer thin slices*

Chopped fresh dill

Roll the pastry out as thinly as possible and use it to line either patty tins or barquette cases. Line each pastry case with greaseproof paper and put a few dried beans on top. Cook for 15 minutes in an oven pre-heated to 350°F/Gas 4.

When the pastry cases are cooked remove the beans and the paper and put the cases back into the oven for a few moments to dry out then leave them to cool.

Fill each barquette or pastry case with thinly sliced salmon, topped with slices of quails' egg and finished with a layer of lemon mayonnaise. Garnish with chopped dill and thin slivers of lemon.

Dips are perfectly acceptable too, provided that you have a really reliable vehicle for scooping them up. I find that prawn crackers are ideal – not too crumbly or flaky and curly enough to hold a decent mouthful. They can be fried well in advance and kept in an airtight tin until served.

CAVIAR DIP WITH PRAWN CRACKERS

4 oz jar caviar

8 oz packet cream cheese

2 tbsp mayonnaise

Very finely chopped onion or scallion to taste

Juice of 1/2 lemon

Dash of tabasco

Dash of Worcester sauce

Milk for consistency, 2 or 3 tbsp

2 hard boiled eggs, finely chopped

Paprika

Prawn Crackers

Combine the cream cheese, mayonnaise, milk, tabasco and Worcester sauce using a food processor or mixing by hand until they are creamily amalgamated.

Spread in a dish (a large glass fingerbowl looks well) and cover with caviar.

Sprinkle with lemon juice and finish off with a layer of chopped onions and eggs and a dusting of paprika.

Put the bowl containing the dip on a serving tray and pile the prawn crackers round it.

But in this bibulous country, they're here for the beer. Seasonal drinks parties can get into a rut and Christmas can be particularly deadly. Even the most dedicated junkie becomes caramelised after twelve nights of mulled wine and mince pies. If you want to give the cheapest party of the year, January the First is a great date. At least half of your guests will have foresworn the demon drink and the rest will feel too fragile to make much of a hole in your stocks. However, one drink that will soothe even the most sated palate is…

CHRISTMAS EGG NOG

8 eggs

½ lb castor sugar

½ bottle Bourbon (Four Roses or similar)

4 fl oz brown rum

1 pint thick cream

2 pints milk

Separate the eggs into two basins.

Add the sugar to the basin with the egg whites and gently beat until the sugar is dissolved but the egg white is not stiff.

Put this mixture into a blender and add the yolks and, finally, the rum. Pour this mixture into a large bowl and gently whisk in the milk, cream and Bourbon.

When all the ingredients are thoroughly combined, chill for a few hours in the fridge.

Serve in a punch bowl and ladle into syllabub cups, dusting the top of each serving with a little grated fresh nutmeg.

For more intimate groups, the old fashioned 'thirties cocktail kick-start can create a great mood. Once again, do not be too totalitarian. Allow people to opt out if they want to. Black Velvet with oysters makes a stylish start to a day at the races, whilst a White Lady makes a wonderful prelude to an evening at the theatre. I still remember Nigel O'Flaherty celebrating the first hot Sunday morning of the summer a few years ago with a Mint Julep party in his home overlooking Killiney Bay. Serve this following trio with macadamia or cashew nuts, quails' eggs and extreme caution.

BLACK VELVET

Take a tall 12 ounce tumbler and pour in 8 fluid ounces of Guinness. When that has settled, gently top with champagne.

WHITE LADY

In a shaker mix 1 measure of gin, $1/2$ measure of Cointreau and $1/3$ measure of fresh lemon juice with a good handful of ice and shake until slightly frothy.

Serve with a maraschino cherry or two on a silver stick.

MINT JULEP

Take 4-5 sprigs of mint, half a tablespoon of very fine sugar and 1 tablespoon water. Crush all these together until the sugar is completely dissolved and the flavour of the mint is extracted.

Take a 12 ounce tumbler and frost the rim by moistening and then dipping quickly in castor sugar.

Strain the sugar, mint and water mixture into the tumbler and add 2 fluid ounces of Bourbon.

Fill the glass to the top with crushed ice and stir well to frost the outside of the tumbler. Decorate with a sprig of mint and serve with two drinking straws.

If it's a drinks party for two and you're looking for courting cocktails I swear by these two seductive tipples.

WHISKY SOUR

Mix 1 measure of Scotch whisky, $1/_2$ measure of fresh lemon juice, $1/_2$ measure of lemon squash and the white of one egg in a cocktail shaker with small ice cubes and shake until the egg white is foamy.

This cocktail is every bit as smooth and sensuous as it sounds but one pair of these stockings is enough for anyone who doesn't want to end up legless or indeed stockingless.

SILKEN STOCKINGS

Use an electric blender to whizz up; 2 parts blonde rum, 2 parts crème de cacao, 2 parts fresh cream, and a dash of grenadine, with a good scoop of crushed ice.

Pour into tall, frosted glasses and use cinnamon to dust the surface very lightly.

However much people profess to loathe cocktail parties it looks as though they will be with us for the moment, so next time you are balancing on your stilettos, juggling bag, glass and canapé and (in my case) trying to light a cigarette, just remember that: 'The human comedy begins with a vertical smile,' and smile on through.

The Lost Weekend

'The first day a guest, the second day a guest, the third day a calamity.'
Indian proverb.

Max Beerbohm memorably described hosts and guests as tyrants and tyrannised. Many a hostess, exhausted by her efforts to entertain curmudgeonly house guests might feel Beerbohm got it the wrong way round. The most successful long haul hostess has to combine the firmness of a benevolent despot with the charm of Pamela Harriman. A lifetime of dining with friends can leave one totally unprepared for the sort of idiosyncracies which people exhibit once they are resident in your house.

A weekend hostess who does not homogenise her group is apt to end up with nervous prostration. Nothing illustrates this quite so pointedly as the house party. People who have fled to the countryside in search of pastoral peace are aghast when a later arrival unpacks two noisy terriers and a guitar from her car. After dinner the bridge faction and the charades enthusiasts can almost come to blows. Sportsmen seem like a pretty safe bet as they're out from first light trying to kill things but they need a tremendous amount of valeting and sympathy when they return soaked, muddy, torn and possibly empty-handed. Golfers talk about it ad nauseum, usually to people who are only interested in the more obscure topography of the district and who have already uncovered humiliating depths of ignorance in this department in their resident hosts.

On the whole, the honest hedonist is probably the easiest visitor. They come punctually to meals, and rest a lot. They are as contented and undemanding as sea slugs as long as they have somewhere comfortable to loll about between trips to the trough (unsurprisingly I fall into this category) but even they can get cranky if the food is sparse or nasty. The finest architecture in the province will not console them if the hostess has managed to stretch a pound of mince and a head of chicory between ten people.

The ideal mood to orchestrate at the beginning of a long weekend is one of delightful expectation. Don't bring all your big guns to bear on the first night but adopt similar principles to the marriage feast of Cana where the best things were held in reserve until the last. Local lions (if you are fortunate enough to have any) should be held back until the guests have either bonded or become bored enough to enjoy meeting the woman who delivered her own baby on a raft or the bloke who rode a jennet from Tierra del Fuego to Alaska.

On Friday evening start very simply with just a hint or two of treats in store. Plan a plain and hearty main dish which will still taste good if people are delayed on the drive or held up at the office – something like Boston Baked Beans with crusty breads and crisp salads.

Terry Keane enjoying lobster in West Cork, Summer '93.

Raymond Blanc, chef/patron of Le Manoir aux Quat' Saisons, lunching with Terry Keane in Le Mistral, Dublin, Summer '94. Photograph: Colm Henry.

Party at Christmas '93. L to R: Julie Campbell, Alfred Cochrane, Terry Keane, Gordon Campbell. Photograph: Colm Henry.

Cartoons by Jim Cogan for Terry Keane's Tabletalk column in the
Sunday Independent *with Ann Madden and Louis le Brocquy, Jeffrey Bernard,*
Brendan Kennelly and Joan Collins.

Lunching with Mas D'Artigny near Saint-Paul in the South of France, Summer '90 with L to R: Louis le Brocquy, Terry Keane, Ann Madden and Harry Sydner.

Lunching with Roger Verge in his restaurant Moulin de Mougins on the Côte d'Azur in the South of France during the making of the series France à la Carte for RTE.

Wine tasting in Stellenbosch region outside Cape Town, South Africa, Winter '94.

Party given for Buzz Aldrin, the second man on the moon, L to R:
Julie Campbell, Buzz Aldrin, Gordon Campbell.

Christmas '90 at home. L to R: Christian Bauer, Ann O' Donnell (mother), Madeleine Keane (daughter), John Burke (standing), Terry Keane, Timothy Keane (son), Jane de Boer (daughter, standing), Karl Carpenter (son-in-law), Mary Gibbons, Natasha Keane (granddaughter). Photograph by Colm Henry

BOSTON BAKED BEANS

1 lb dried haricot beans

8 oz smoked streaky bacon in one piece

2 medium onions, chopped

2 cloves garlic, chopped

2 tbsp molasses

2 tbsp prepared mustard (English)

2 tsp grated ginger root

1 tin chopped tomatoes

Bay-leaf, thyme and winter savory to taste

2 oz brown sugar

Soak the beans overnight before draining and putting in a saucepan with about 4 pints of cold water.

Simmer until the beans are just *al dente*. Drain and reserve the liquid.

Cut the bacon into 1/2 inch cubes and sauté in a frying pan.

Add the onions and garlic and soften. Put the drained beans, bacon, onion, garlic and all other ingredients into a casserole dish and mix well.

Add enough of the cooking liquid to cover the mixture and bake in a slow oven (300-350°F/Gas 2-3) for about three hours.

A dash of ketchup or vinegar can be added to taste before serving.

For years I've been the lucky recipient of Gill Bowler's consummate hospitality. She recommends a triple measure drink by the fire as soon as her guests arrive with something to be nibbled in the hand such as warm toast, ready spread with paté, small *dolmades* or radishes with a basket of baguettes. On summer evenings she puts her arrivals into comfortable chairs on the terrace or beside the pool for their drink and serves quails' eggs with coarse salt, a *tortilla* cut in cubes (see *Tippling into Temptation* p.62) or roasted pepper salad with French bread.

GILL BOWLER'S ROASTED PEPPER SALAD

Pre-heat the oven to 400°F/Gas 6 and roast red or yellow peppers for about 15 minutes, turning them after 7 minutes. They should be soft and slightly blackened by this time. Allow them to cool and then peel away the skin, remove the seeds and cut into strips.

Pack tightly into a screw-top container and top up to the brim with olive oil.

This will keep in the fridge for up to six weeks and is delicious on its own with just good bread or as an accompaniment to charcuterie or Greek salad.

Other summer salads for the pool-side which Gill recommends are *Salade Niçoise*, with tuna, olives and anchovies or tomato salad with onion and basil. On fine summer weekends when guests tend to drift out into the garden with their pre-prandial drinks, it is a good idea to have the makings of Kir, Kir Royale or Pimms on hand. A tall jug of Pimms on a fine summer evening seems as right as an applewood fire in January. Just remember that with these cocktails, less is always more. When you make Pimms leave your fruit and veg to be admired where they belong – in the kitchen garden or on the table. They should not be hacked up and turned into a saturated fruit salad masquerading as a cocktail. A twist of citron zest and a sprig of borage are the only acceptable garnish for Pimms. Similarly, when mixing Kir or Kir Royale the merest hint of *cassis* should suffice. You must never serve your guests a drink which looks like arterial blood and tastes like Ribena. Give the wine a chance to speak for itself.

Throughout the 'eighties Ulli and Brian de Breffny hosted magical weekends at their beautiful home Castletown Cox. Guests came from all over the world to enjoy their superb hospitality. Writers, artists, architects and ambassadors and well-known figures from the world of music, bloodstock and fine arts mingled happily and enjoyed the eclectic atmosphere and the pampering. Many lasting friendships were made in that enchanted environment. Friday evening supper always took place in the vaulted basement kitchen with its massive pine furniture and copper saucepans originating from one of the Hapsburg palaces.

One of Ulli's simple supper dishes, equally suitable for an informal lunch, is her Pasta Puttanesca. I am at a loss to know why this dish is attributed to the ladies of the night – perhaps because it is so simple to make that even a hard working girl can find time to prepare and enjoy it. Ulli and her inimitable *aide de camp*, Mavis Keegan, the genie of the basement kitchen, always use their own pasta machine for this dish but a good quality ready-made pasta such as Napolina Frills will make an excellent substitute.

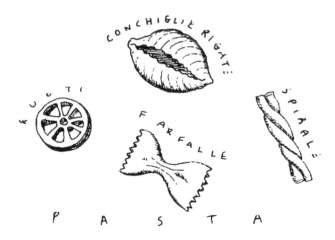

ULLI'S PASTA PUTTANESCA
(serves 4-6)

For the sauce:

2 cloves garlic, crushed

1 puréed raw onion

1 tin chopped tomatoes

2 tins anchovies, chopped finely

A good dash of tabasco sauce

A pinch of chilli pepper(just enough to cover the tip of a fingernail)

A walnut of butter

2-3 tbsp olive oil

Gently sauté the garlic and onion in the butter and olive oil for about five minutes on a low heat.

Add the chopped tomatoes, chilli and tabasco and continue to cook a little longer. Finally add the coarsely chopped anchovies and continue cooking for a further few minutes.

This sauce can be made well ahead of time. In fact, the flavours infuse better the longer it is resting.

FOR THE PASTA

If you are using commercially made pasta, cook according to the directions on the packet.

For your own home-made pasta just allow 3-4 minutes in fast boiling water with salt and oil.

Stir the sauce through when you are ready to serve.

A good robust accompaniment to this is Rosso di Montalcino (the Campo al Sassi is very good indeed).

On Saturday evenings, when dinner was served in the dignified surroundings of the de Breffni dining-room, there was often a magnificent fish dish as the central feature of the meal. Seeing this flaming sea bass carried into the room by Kishin, the butler, was a memorable experience. The sea bass selected for this dish should be between 4 and 7 pounds in weight. A fish smaller than 4 pounds tends to have too soft a backbone and this makes the preparation difficult. A fish larger than 7 pounds could constitute a challenge to your cooking and serving dishes.

♂EA BA♂♂ FLAMBÉ

*1 sea bass, circa
5-6 lb weight*

For the stuffing:

2 lb lemon sole

1 lb fennel root

*2 oz white
breadcrumbs*

*2 tsp powdered
bay-leaf*

Juice of 2 lemons

*Pepper and salt to
taste*

*4 tbsp brandy to
flambé the finished
dish*

Split the skin and flesh of the raw sea bass down the line of the backbone. Take out the backbone and smaller bones through the split at the top.

Cook the fennel root until it is soft. While it is cooking skin the raw lemon sole.

When the fennel is cooked allow it to cool and then make a purée of the fennel, the raw sole and the white breadcrumbs. Shake the powdered bay-leaf, pepper and salt into this mixture and stir. Put the stuffing into the cavity which has been made by removing the backbone of the sea bass.

Close the flesh of the sea bass over the stuffing and secure with cocktail sticks. Wrap the stuffed fish in 2 layers of tinfoil with the juice of the two lemons. Do not add any butter or oil. Poach the wrapped fish in a large *bain-marie* in the oven.

(Mavis Keegan's husband manufactured a bass shaped *bain-marie* for this dish but it can be cooked on a trivet over a roasting pan half filled with water instead.) About $3/4$ of an hour at a medium heat (350-375°F/Gas 4-5) should be enough for this dish depending upon the size of the bass.

To flambé for serving, heat the brandy in a small pan until it is bubbling then pour over the fish on the serving dish and set alight immediately.

This magnificent dish deserves a good Rhone white such as a Coindreau ideally from Guigal or Chave, or the white Mas Daumas Gassac. If you are not feeling that flush Guigal's white Côte du Rhone is a very adequate substitute.

Lobster sauce, so often, is a thin pink glaze which has, at some stage in its manufacture, had a long-dead lobster shell waved over the pan. The lobster sauce served in Castletown with delicately poached turbot was luscious perfection.

TURBOT WITH LOBSTER SAUCE

4 lb turbot

1 large (3 lb) or 2 small (1½ lb each) lobsters

Juice of 1½ lemons

4 oz butter, melted

Herbs; bouquet garni (1 sachet if dried), and any other suitable fresh herbs (dill, fennel etc.) which you have available

Hollandaise sauce to finish

Wrap the turbot in a good thick double layer of tinfoil. Baste it with the melted butter and the lemon juice and spread with the herbs before sealing up the foil tightly. Cook in the oven, either in a suitably sized *bain-marie* or on a griddle set over a roasting tin half full of water.

Give the turbot about ¾ of an hour in a medium oven (350°F/Gas 4). In the meantime cook the lobster.

Make sure that it is still lively before you start the cooking process. Mavis recommends stroking their tails to calm them down. Less tender hearted cooks might lid the pan tightly and weight it well to prevent the panic attacks from spreading around the kitchen.

Start the lobsters off in cool water and gradually bring to the boil. Keep at a slow boil for about 10 minutes and let them rest in the hot water for another 15 minutes. Take the lobster meat out of the shell and cut into bite sized cubes.

When the turbot has been cooked and unwrapped and put on a serving plate, arrange the cubed lobster over it and top with Hollandaise sauce.

A good Burgundy marries well with this dish, preferably a St Romain from Jean Germain or a St Véran from Roger Luquet. Another pleasant complement would be a New World, barrel fermented Chardonnay from the Rothbury estate.

Mavis Keegan recommends the Magimix recipe for this sauce as it never fails her. If you do not have a Magimix simply try the following method.

HOLLANDAISE SAUCE

Whisk 4 egg yolks with 4 teaspoons of warm water in the top of a double boiler.

Keep the bottom part of the boiler simmering while slowly adding 8 ounces of unsalted butter. Do not allow the sauce to boil.

When it has thickened season with fresh lemon juice and add salt and pepper to taste.

Another unforgettable dish which preceded many a feast in the Castletown dining-room was salmon stuffed pancakes.

SALMON STUFFED PANCAKES

For filling

1 lb smoked salmon, sliced and chopped roughly

3-4 oz of best creamery butter, melted

Make a pancake batter by combining $1/2$ pound of flour, 3 eggs and $1/2$ a pint of milk. Set the batter aside to stand for at least one hour.

This should make a minimum of one dozen pancakes.

Brush each pancake with the hot melted butter.

Cover with smoked salmon pieces and roll up. Put the pancakes on a serving dish, coat with Hollandaise sauce (see previous recipe) and brown lightly under a grill.

Tea is a rather grey area at weekend parties. Serving tea formally at four or so makes the day into an endless drudgery for anyone who has just finished clearing lunch and is bracing themselves to cook dinner. On the other hand lots of people get withdrawal symptoms if they don't get their afternoon Lapsang/Earl Grey fix. Ulli's solution was to make tea in the afternoons a flexible affair. Those who wanted an early tea before a pre-dinner snooze or those who came in later than intended after a long walk just helped themselves. This is a good, uncomplicated cake for tea-time grazers.

TEA BRACK

6 oz each of:
raisins, sultanas,
brown sugar and
plain flour

6 fl oz strong black tea

1 egg

1 tsp baking powder

1 tsp mixed spice (optional)

Dissolve the sugar thoroughly in the tea then add the dried fruit and leave to soak overnight.

Next day beat the egg and fold it in alternately with the sifted flour into the soaked fruit mixture.

Finally add the baking powder and the spice, if required.

Put into a loaf tin lined with greaseproof paper and cook at about 300°F/Gas 2 for about an hour and a half.

The brack is cooked when a skewer inserted into the centre comes out clean.

Stout can be substituted for some or all of the tea if you wish to try a more richly flavoured version.

Bracks keep well in airtight tins.

When game is in season it always seems to taste much better in the country, where appetites have been sharpened by outdoor exercise, or at least by clean air. The problem with enthusiastic home shooting is that it can result in too mixed a bag to give everybody the brace of snipe, half pheasant or whatever. The solution to dealing with these potentially interesting mixes is, of course, game pie. Its other advantage is that you can gouge away and remove every last bit of shot in deference to those guests with fillings in their teeth. Once the beasts are going into a pastry crust it does not matter if they look a little mangled.

GAME FOR ANYTHING PIE (COLD)

For pastry:

12 oz plain flour

1 egg yolk

4 tbsp milk

4 tbsp water

3 oz lard

Pinch salt

Sift the flour and salt into a warmed bowl and make a well in the centre.

Beat the yolk with one tablespoon of milk and pour into the well. Heat the remaining milk, water, butter and lard slowly in a saucepan until boiling.

Add this to the mixture in the well and then mix all together thoroughly. Knead until smooth and then leave to rest for half an hour in a cloth covered basin over a pan of warm water. Roll it out while it is still warm.

FOR THE FILLING:

This obviously will vary depending on what is available.

Basically you will need about 28 ounces of raw, boneless game meat – venison, pheasant, pigeon, hare, mallard, rabbit etc.

The game meat can be supplemented with a half pound or so of chopped beef steak. Some people prefer to add a little steak anyway to reduce the overall richness of the dish. If venison predominates add a dozen juniper berries. Chopped chestnuts are good with pheasant and a smear of redcurrant jelly will enhance pigeon breasts.

Slice all the meat into strips and marinate in a glass of port, a dash of brandy, a few fluid ounces of olive oil and a few crushed peppercorns for at least two hours before making up the pie.

FOR ASSEMBLING THE PIE:

Roll out two thirds of the pastry and use to line a greased, loose-bottomed cake tin (about 8 inches in diameter).

For filling:

8 oz sausage meat

4 oz diced rashers

1 grated onion

½ pint rich stock

1 tsp chopped herbs

1 beaten egg

1 sachet of gelatine

Line the base of the pastry with a layer of sausage meat.

Mix the marinated game meat with the diced rashers, grated onion, herbs and whatever other flavourings you are using (chestnuts, juniper berries etc.) and half of the stock.

Put all this into the pie case and then roll out the remaining pastry and cover the pie, moistening the edges to make a good seal; Decorate and brush with beaten egg, make a hole in the top about ½ an inch in diameter.

Cover the top with greased paper to prevent burning. Stand the pie on a baking tray and put into a hot oven, 400°F/Gas 6 for about half an hour, then reduce the heat to 300°F/Gas 2 for a further 2 hours.

When the pie is cooked, dissolve the gelatine in the remaining stock and pour into the hole in the lid of the pie.

Leave in the tin for at least 12 hours before taking out and serving. Serve with Cumberland sauce or orange salad.

Another wonderful warm game dish for winter weekends is jugged hare. The classic jug hare is made with the reserved blood of the beast. There are times when the jug of blood proves elusive. When you have put several hares in your freezer it is unlikely that you will have reserved blood for all of them. Also if a friend gives you a hare ready dressed or you buy one in from your game supplier it usually comes without a tupperware container of body fluids. This hare recipe, however, does not require the blood and still tastes rich and delicious without it.

JUGGED HARE
(serves 8-10)

A 5-6 lb hare, fresh or frozen

25 fl oz red wine

1 large sliced onion

2 tbsp olive oil

3-4 whole juniper berries crushed

3 bay-leaves

1 tbsp chopped parsley

1 tsp chopped dried rosemary

1 tsp chopped dried thyme

8 oz bacon, in the piece, coarsely diced

A few finely chopped shallots

3 or 4 sticks of chopped celery

5 or 6 small, chopped carrots

2 tbsp flour

3 tbsp redcurrant jelly

1 tsp coarsely ground salt

Freshly ground pepper

(If you have managed to reserve a smidgeon of the hare blood you can add about half a cup to this recipe but it is not essential.)

Put the wine, oil, onion, juniper berries, 1 bay-leaf, rosemary, sprinkle of salt and black pepper into a mixing bowl.

Wash the hare well in cold water and dry it, then cut the flesh into 2 inch strips and put into the mixing bowl to marinate.

Turn it from time to time, keeping it in a cool place or in the refrigerator for a minimum of six hours.

When the marinating process is complete, drain the hare meat and set aside.

Reserve the marinade, discarding the onions and herbs.

Dry the pieces of hare with kitchen paper and coat lightly with flour.

Fry the bacon dice in the olive oil until it is crisp and well coloured.

Take it out with a slotted spoon and set aside then brown the hare meat in the fat in which you have already cooked the bacon.

Set the hare aside with the bacon and use the fat to cook the shallots, celery and carrots for 5 to 10 minutes over a gentle heat until they are soft but not too browned.

Take a suitably sized casserole dish and put into it the bacon, hare meat, shallots, celery, carrots, the olive oil used in the frying and the reserved marinade.

Add the redcurrant jelly (and the blood if available) and mix together well with the thyme, parsley, two remaining bay-leaves, 1/2 tsp of salt and a little ground pepper.

Cover the casserole tightly and braise at 350°F/Gas 4 for about an hour until the hare is tender.

This is a rich dish and will not overpower a Mas Daumas Gassac. Alternatively try an Eileen Hardy Reserve Shiraz from Languedoc or a Cornas.

No country weekend is complete without the opportunity to sin outrageously – at least on the calorie stakes. An indulgent and irresistible treat for chocaholics is a Chocolate Roulade.

CHOCOLATE ROULADE

6 oz Chocolate Menier

5 eggs

6 oz castor sugar

3 tbsp hot water

½ pint cream

Icing sugar for dredging

Melt the chocolate in a *bain-marie* and separate the eggs. Beat the yolks with the sugar until pale and creamy.

Stir the hot water into the melted chocolate and then add the egg yolk and sugar mixture. Whisk the egg-whites and fold in.

Oil a biscuit tin measuring about 14 inches x 9 inches and line with a double layer of oiled greaseproof paper.

Pour the mixture into this tin and bake in a moderate oven – 350°F/Gas 4 – for about 15 minutes. Remove the chocolate mousse from the oven and set aside, covered with a sheet of oiled greaseproof paper and a damp cloth.

Allow to cool for a short while. When it is still warm but not hot, take off the cloth and the greaseproof paper and turn it out onto a fresh sheet of greaseproof paper well dusted with icing sugar and a little larger than the mousse itself.

Use the greaseproof paper to roll the mousse gently into a log shape, like a Swiss Roll.

Leave it covered until it is cool. It can be left overnight at this stage if you wish.

Unroll it gently and spread with stiffly whipped cream. Re-roll and dust with icing sugar.

Only the brave or foolish serve anything potable with chocolate, but fortune favours the brave and it was my good luck to get these tips from Declan Ryan. They work. Chocolate roulade tastes even better with a glass of Banyuls red, Domain de la Rectorie, or Wilm Peche de Vigne liqueur.

Ultimately if you insist on torturing yourself and inviting a houseparty, do your homework beforehand. Even the most accomplished hostesses will find it impossible to cater for half a dozen different tastes. As George Bernard Shaw expounded: 'Do not do unto others as you would they should do unto you. Their tastes might not be the same.'

Life is a Picnic

'Sand in the sandwiches, wasps in the tea,
Sun on our bathing dresses heavy with the wet,
Squelch of the bladder wrack waiting for the sea
Fleas round the Tamarisk, an early cigarette.'
John Betjeman.

In this so-called temperate climate one is lucky if gritty sandwiches and a few superfluous insects are the worst things encountered when feeding alfresco. Icy winds and torrential rain can ambush one at any point in the calendar and, if the temperature creeps up sufficiently for a hatch of fly, the day can degenerate into what Somerville and Ross described as 'midge bitten misery'.

However, school sports days, gymkhanas, country race meetings, the hatching of the mayfly and a host of other perennial events can all necessitate a dinner *e mobile* being packed in the car boot. At many of these venues the food has to be unpacked and consumed in front of a shamelessly nosy group of peers.

It is extraordinary how picnickers who are not actually responsible for making and packing the meal seem to dislike the shabby-chic of a few jam sambos and a flask of tea. My formula is to go for a robustly flavoured main dish, crisp salads, the firmest cheeses and fruits and to make sure that anything sweet that is handed round with the coffee is not too sticky. I avoid anything in aspic or mayonnaise because, if the sun does break through, the consequences can be disastrously slimy. Nobody can be on top form with molten aspic down the front of their Armani and snail trails of mayonnaise on the Hermès handbag.

If you are having your *déjeuner sur l'herbe* it is more than likely that most of your wine will end up *sur l'herbe* as well. Having been shaken, if not stirred, in the car boot it will then be leaked, kicked over, spilt and dropped in the ensuing melée.

Waste not, want not is my motto. We are assured that everything tastes better in the open air so this is the time to rake the shelves for the cheapest plonk. I will refrain from naming or shaming bottlers or importers and maintain that even their produce can be served with style.

A swift-running mountain stream is romantic but not always a viable option as a cooling system. Most prosaically effective is a thick layer of coarse, wet muslin wrapped around the bottles which are then left in a draught.

This is the nineteenth century forerunner of modern refrigeration. The subsequent evaporation will cool the wine down several degrees below the ambient temperature.

An all weather favourite of mine for outdoor eating is a firm country terrine. The texture and flavour seem to be particularly appropriate for picnics and it carries and cuts well.

TERRY'S TERRINE

1 lb minced belly pork

1 lb minced veal (chicken breasts can be substituted if veal is not available)

1 lb minced pig's liver

1 glass dry white wine

1 standard measure of brandy

20 green or black peppers, crushed coarsely

4 cloves garlic, crushed

4 oz streaky rashers

Combine all of these ingredients except the rashers, and leave to stand for a few hours.

Cut the rind off half of the rashers and arrange them in the bottom of a terrine dish.

Dice the remaining rashers and the discarded rinds and stir them into the mixture then pour it into the terrine dish.

Put the dish into a roasting tin half filled with water and cook, uncovered, in a pre-heated low oven 300°F/Gas 2, for about $1^3/_4$ -2 hours, making sure that the water surrounding the dish does not steam dry.

It is cooked when the sides of the meat mixture shrink away from the sides of the tin.

Cover the top of the *terrine* with greaseproof paper and leave it well weighted down overnight so that it will set firmly and slice well.

Turn it out the following day by loosening the sides with a knife and dipping the base of the tin briefly into boiling water.

A screw-top jar of port wine jelly can be taken as an optional extra with this dish. The more smartly dressed or less dextrous can always pass on it but it enhances the terrine wonderfully. It is also good with cold ham, hot mutton and most game dishes. If the weather gets really horrible you could always point out that any port in a storm is better than none!

PORTABLE PORT

4 tbsp
redcurrant jelly

1 tsp Dijon mustard

1 tsp very finely
grated root ginger

Juice and finely
grated rind of 1
orange and ½ lemon

6 fl oz port

1 sachet of gelatine

Heat all these ingredients except the gelatine slowly in a pan.

Do not allow to boil but stir gently until all the ingredients are amalgamated.

Set aside for about ten minutes then dissolve the gelatine in two tablespoons of boiling water.

Stir the gelatine mixture through the port wine mixture. Pour into a heated screw-top jar and leave to set.

A Waldorf salad complements this richly flavoured pork dish perfectly. It will not get limp in transit and needs only the lightest dressing as the dill and lemon juice add plenty of character.

WALDORF SALAD

Equal quantities of;
apples, (preferably
Cox's pippins)

Celery sticks (from
the inner part of the
head)

Grapes, small and
seedless

The juice of ½
lemon

Dill seeds to taste

Walnuts (½ amount
of any of the above
ingredients)

Wash celery, apples and grapes.

Core the apples and cut in quarters, without peeling.

Dice the apples into ½ inch cubes and sprinkle with lemon juice.

Cut the celery stalks to the same size and add the grapes and the coarsely crumbled walnuts.

Toss in a small amount of dressing, just enough to give a slight coating to the vegetables without masking the flavour.

Scatter dill seeds to taste.

Quiches are excellent picnic fare too. They travel well and are easy to serve in informal surroundings. As the following quiche contains shellfish be sure to transport it in a cool box or Thermos bag and do not leave it out in the sun before serving. Don't believe that real men won't eat it. In my experience they devour this one.

CRAB QUICHE

For the pastry
4 oz plain flour
½ tsp mustard powder
Pinch cayenne pepper
2½ oz butter
2 oz grated cheese (mature Cheddar or Gruyère)
1 egg yolk
2-3 tsp cold water
Pinch salt

First make the pastry.

Sift the flour, mustard and cayenne with the pinch of salt.

Cut in the butter and rub in well. Add the cheese and toss.

Mix to a stiff paste with the egg yolk and water.

Knead on a lightly floured board until smooth and then leave to rest in the fridge for at least half an hour.

Roll out and use to line a greased 8" flan dish.

For the filling
6 oz crab body meat
5 fl oz milk
5 fl oz cream
3 beaten eggs
10-12 peeled prawns
1 oz grated cheese
Salt and black pepper

To make the filling, heat the milk and cream to just below boiling point then combine with the beaten eggs. Season with salt and pepper.

Spread the crabmeat over the base of the flan case.

Pour the egg and milk mix over then sprinkle grated cheese and arrange the prawns on top.

Put into an oven pre-heated to 400°F/Gas 6 and after five minutes or so reduce heat to 325°F/Gas 3.

Bake until the filling is well set. This should take about 35-45 minutes in all.

Where it is not possible to take plates and cutlery, in a small boat, for example, or on a long hike, real finger food is essential. Crusty rolls, which are an essential part of a picnic should be buttered before they are packed. I always do this as a slab of butter on a warm day is as hazardous as aspic. These spiced beef rolls are very good to eat and not at all treacherous.

Spiced Beef Rolls

5 wafer thin slices spiced beef

If using fresh asparagus, trim off all the woody growth after cooking and draining.

5 slices Parma ham

Roll up each asparagus spear in a half slice of Parma ham then in a half slice of spiced beef.

10 asparagus spears, tinned, bottled or fresh and pre-cooked

Secure with toothpicks.

It is all too easy to slide into a rut over family picnics, so do check up on everyone's current preferences. Ordinary family meals change imperceptibly with burgeoning ages and fluctuating tastes but picnics are rare enough to become set in a sort of ersatz tradition, like flies in amber. I slavishly made Scotch eggs for every picnic that I packed for my children, in the erroneous belief that they would be devastated not to see this family favourite appearing from the hamper. Only now that they are all adults do they feel able to tell me that they loathed the beastly things and struggled through them out of consideration for my feelings. The coastline of Ireland is mined with the ones they buried when I wasn't looking.

Good firm cheese and fruit with a few designer biscuits (not chocolate) are, more often than not, all that people feel like when other activities are on the cards but one superlative pudding which survives the car boot and the picnic basket is *Gâteau Pithiviers*.

GÂTEAU PITHIVIERS

¼ lb ground almonds

¼ lb powdered sugar

2 eggs

3½ tbsp melted butter

6 tbsp brown rum

1 packet puff pastry

Mix the sugar, almonds and one egg to make a smooth paste. Add the rum and melted butter and leave to cool for at least half an hour.

Take one third of the puff pastry and roll into a circle about 8 inches in diameter before rolling remaining pastry into a larger circle of about 10-11 inches diameter and slightly thicker than the first circle.

Spread the frangipane mixture that you have made from the almonds etc. onto the larger circle of pastry. Wet the edge and slash it in 1 inch diagonals round the perimeter.

Place the smaller circle of pastry on top and fold the slashed edge over it to make a good seal.

Leave a small hole in the centre of the pie to allow the steam from cooking to escape. Beat the remaining egg and brush it onto the pie.

Place in an oven pre-heated to 400°F/Gas 6 for 40 minutes.

Dredge with icing sugar and serve either warm or cold with whipped cream if desired.

Another delicious cold picnic dish, which I discovered by happy accident, is *Poulet W.H. Auden*. It is normally served as a hot dinner dish, and very delicious it is, but I happened to taste *les restes* one day and thought that this dish was even more succulent cold.

Michael O'Sullivan, who cooked this dish for me, was introduced to it at a party of Leonard Bernstein's in Vienna. It had first been invented in New York in honour of W.H. Auden by the librettist, Chester Kallman (the writer of *The Rake's Progress* for Stravinsky). This chicken is infinitely more digestible than its pedigree!

POULET W.H. AUDEN
(serves 6)

6 chicken breasts (part boned)

Skin the chicken breasts and rub the meat with garlic, rosemary, salt and pepper.

6 fresh oranges

2 wine glasses of dessert wine

Make a marinade by squeezing the juice of the six oranges into an ovenproof dish and adding some finely grated peel to the liquid.

2 cloves garlic, crushed

Add the two glasses of dessert wine and the bay-leaf.

A sprig of rosemary

A bay-leaf

Put the meat in the marinade and leave it in a cool place overnight. Cook for 35-40 minutes at 400°F/Gas 6.

Salt and black pepper to taste

Garnish with slices of fresh orange.

For a hostess, a barbecue is somehow less exigent than a picnic. The commitment is at a different level. For one thing there is one's own roof nearby if the weather, or anything else, turns ugly and a retreat is in order. Much more important than this is the fact that cooking things over charcoal seems to have become a male preserve. Men who have never willingly boiled an egg seem quite happy to wear silly aprons, kipper themselves in charcoal smoke, and fight the fat fires with libations of bottled beer. They seem to think that it is all great fun and I am perfectly happy to go along with this idea as I relax in the sunshine with a chilled Bellini (one dash of Archer's peach liqueur mixed with a glass of champagne or a sparkling dry wine such as Frascati).

Happy though one is to let the chaps get on with it one must admit that quality and consistency leave a certain something to be desired in this method of cooking. On one memorable occasion, in the South of France, I was lounging in the dappled shade of a vine covered terrace, drink in hand, while the men slaved over the hot spit. Sharing the pergola and the frosted drinks with me was a Rather Important Irishwoman. Eventually lunch appeared. A surprisingly succulent kebab, lambently golden and fragrant was handed to me. We had been waiting some time for this moment and my illustrious companion cast a keenly appreciative eye upon it. Seconds later a blackened burlesque of the same thing was handed to her. She looked at it in tragic silence for a moment and then said, sadly, 'In my father's house there are many mansions.' That illustrates, I suppose, why barbecues can be seen as an analogy of the human condition; some are luckier than others. She went on to greater things and I went on to greater barbecues.

These are my tips for a better barbie: be generous with the charcoal, light the fire well in advance of cooking, and start cooking only when a good ash bed has formed. If you are away from your regular butcher, and not too sure about the quality of the meat, a commercial meat tenderiser might be a sensible addition. But the best plan with barbecued food is to marinate everything for as long as possible. Cooking uncovered, over charcoal, can make meat tougher as well as tastier and marinades, based on honey, soy sauce, wine, herbs and spices will add enormously to the enjoyment of the finished dish. Always turn meat in a marinade frequently to ensure even coverage and slash the skins on chicken and other birds. This is a typical all-purpose marinade which can be used for steeping, basting and as a relish for the cooked meat.

All-Purpose Marinade

1 tsp garlic salt
1 tsp ground ginger
1 tsp paprika
4 tbsp clear honey
3 tbsp tomato purée
4 tbsp wine vinegar
Dash Worcester sauce
½ pint rich stock

Combine all these ingredients thoroughly, in a food processor or by hand.

Simmer gently for about ten minutes.

This all-purpose marinade should be left on the meat for as long as possible but will give flavour even if used as a basting sauce.

Kebabs are always terrific at barbecues. They look amusing, are easy to manage and can lend themselves to a variety of dips, rather like fondue. This is a kebab which I have always found successful.

RABELASIAN RUMAKI

1 lb chicken livers
1 lb streaky rashers
1 can water chestnuts

For marinade:
2 fl oz soy sauce; 2 fl oz olive oil; 2 cloves garlic; 2 tbsp ketchup; 2 tbsp wine vinegar; ½ tsp ground pepper; 1 tsp brown sugar

Cut water chestnuts in half and place in the marinade with the livers.

Refrigerate for a minimum of four hours before draining.

Roll up a small piece of liver and half a water chestnut in half of a streaky rasher. Put about 5 or 6 of these small parcels on each skewer and cook until bacon is crispy.

No outdoor griddle is complete without sausages, the thicker the better. Chunky, herbal European sausages taste wonderful when cooked over charcoal. The good old traditional black and white puddings are very good on a barbecue too. Try serving them with apple sauce into which you have stirred a generous handful of French tarragon. If the family still have ketchup dependency you might wean them onto a classier version with this home-made relish.

GREEK STYLE TOMATO SAUCE

Peel and chop 4 large beef tomatoes and add 8 lumps of sugar, 2 crushed cloves of garlic, 4 ounces of minced beef, 1 dessertspoon of finely chopped basil and one large chopped onion. Place in a saucepan and simmer slowly for about 30 minutes.

To conclude an outdoor meal on a blistering, relaxed day nobody really wants a scalding demitasse of rich roast coffee. Iced coffee is the only beverage I take sweetened. It is, from the calorific point of view, an exceedingly wicked drink.

ICED COFFEE

(make 2 pints)

6 tsp good quality instant coffee (Alta Rica, Tasters Choice or similar)

4 level tsp castor sugar

½ pint cold water

½ pint milk

½ pint volume of ice cubes

½ pint cream (if a lighter mix is desired, the cream can be substituted with milk and water mixed 50/50)

6 liqueur measures of Cointreau

Dissolve the coffee and sugar in a few tablespoons of boiling water and stir until the sugar is completely dissolved.

Now add the cold water to this to make up to ½ pint volume and drop in the ice cubes.

When this is done add milk and cream and put the whole mixture into a jug in the fridge. Serve icy cold in tall tumblers with glass or silver drinking straws.

Pour a measure of Cointreau into each tumbler to make a delicious summer post-prandial.

Sit back and delegate.

The point to remember about eating alfresco in Ireland is that we are such a gregarious, sybaritic lot that, if the booze is lavish and the food luscious, no one gives a damn if the heavens open or not. So barbie on down!

The Epicurean Emergency

'Food was a very big factor in Christianity. What would the miracle of the loaves and fishes have been without it?'
Fran Lebowitz, Metropolitan Life.

I've always been consoled by the fact that even Jesus had to put up with unexpected guests. But at least He got a break – none of them were vegetarian. The first prophylactic measure that can be taken against culinary crises is lavish overcatering. Left-overs are far easier to accommodate than the disgruntled guest who is last into a bare buffet.

Sadly the most Lucullan surfeit of good things cannot protect you against the Selective Eater. There are lots of causes for this condition – genuine illnesses, diets, eating disorders and vegetarianism. The last category is the one most likely to cause a problem because, where other selective eaters will pick politely around what is on offer, vegetarians can be absolutely voracious.

Vegans also have a disconcerting habit of forgetting to tell the hostess about their dietary preferences until the last minute. A typical emergency arises when the *foie gras* is sliced, the duck consommé nicely clear and the Beef Wellington approaching gleaming perfection. You open the door to a couple who sniff the air self righteously and say: 'You do know we are vegetarian?' Oddly enough, although I have frequently dined in vegetarian homes, I never open the evening by announcing that I am an enthusiastic carnivore.

The theory is that it's easy to whip up an omelette but only a bad egg would substitute same for supper. Ideally your freezer or store cupboard should yield up some politically correct morsels which can be nuked in the microwave. A jar of vegetarian pesto can make up a quick, acceptable pasta dish. Matty Ryan always keeps a variety of ready stuffed pancakes in his freezer, some with vegetarian fillings such as creamed spinach. In fact, this chapter owes a great deal to Matty's extraordinary ability to cope with unanticipated culinary demands.

If, on the other hand you know in advance that your guests prefer vegetarian food and you have time to prepare for their requirements you could try this superb dish from John Howard of the Coq Hardi, which should delight people of all eating tastes.

JOHN HOWARD'S AUBERGINE CHARLOTTE
(serves 4)

3-4 small aubergines (about 2 pounds weight)

1/4 pint olive oil

1 medium onion, finely chopped

1 clove garlic, crushed

10 tomatoes, peeled chopped and seeded

1/2 pint natural yoghurt

1/4 pint vegetable stock

Salt and freshly ground pepper

Cut the aubergines into half inch slices. Sprinkle with salt and leave for 1/2 an hour to sweat out excess liquid.

Rinse in cold water and dry on a paper towel. Heat 2 tablespoons of olive oil in a saucepan.

Add the finely chopped onion and cook until lightly brown. Add the garlic, tomatoes, salt and pepper and cook for about 20 minutes over a low heat.

Heat the remaining olive oil in a large frying pan and brown the aubergines on both sides.

Arrange a layer of overlapping aubergine slices in the bottom and on the sides of an 8 inch round cake tin. Onto this spread a layer of tomato and then a layer of yoghurt.

Continue with these layers and finish with a layer of aubergine slices. You should reserve about a 1/4 of the tomato mixture for the sauce.

Cover the tin with foil and bake in the oven at 350°F/Gas 4 for 45 minutes.

Cool slightly and unmould onto a serving dish.

Mix the reserve tomato with the stock and bring to the boil.

Adjust the seasoning and pour the sauce around the Charlotte. If I have fresh basil I always use it with the tomato in this dish.

Anthony O'Brien's cooking is every bit as original as his painting, pottery and instrument making. He has a huge repertoire of Indian recipes which he is continually researching and enlarging. Many of them are wonderful dishes to serve to vegetarians, such as this Matarpaneer.

M ATARPANEER

The Paneer:

2 l milk

1 heaped tsp salt

1 tsp freshly ground black pepper

1 tsp whole cummin seed, ground

1/2 tsp ground cardamons

1 Jif squeezy lemon

Put all the ingredients, except the lemon, into a saucepan and bring to the boil, very slowly, stirring continuously.

When the mixture comes to the boil add the whole squeezy lemon. The fluid will start to separate into curds and whey.

Keep it simmering until the separation is quite complete then drain through a sieve which has been lined with a double layer of muslin.

Reserve about a pint of the whey for use later in making the Matar sauce. Screw the muslin up very tightly round the curds and weight it well. It should take about 20-30 minutes to set into a firm curd cheese then it should be sliced into cubes about 1 inch square and deep fried until golden. (If you wish to reserve the deep fried paneer cubes for use the following day they will keep in water, refrigerated. Otherwise they become hard and crumbly.)

The Matar:

3-4 tbsp oil

1 finely chopped onion

2 peeled tomatoes

While the Paneer is setting make the Matar as follows:

Sauté the onion very gently in the oil until it is golden then add the peeled tomatoes and cook to a thick paste.

½ tsp salt

1 tsp coarsely crushed peppercorns

1 small chilli, de-seeded and finely chopped

2 cloves garlic, crushed

1 small piece of root ginger – about 1 inch long, grated

1 tsp turmeric

1 tbsp coriander

½ tsp fenugreek

½ tsp cumin

*2-3 whole **black** cardamons, ground*

A pinch of Chinese curry powder

1 pint whey (from the Paneer)

1 lb frozen peas

At this point add the salt, peppercorns, chilli, garlic and grated ginger and sauté all together for a few minutes.

Then add turmeric, coriander, fenugreek and cumin.

The Chinese spice powder can be added now. Its use is optional but it lends a delicious background scent of fennel to the dish.

Add half a pint of whey from the Paneer, if the sauce is too thick, add a little more and simmer with the frozen peas until they are cooked.

Finally add the cubes of deep fried Paneer and finish with a handful of chopped fresh coriander leaf.

This dish can be supplemented, if you have extra mouths to feed, by cubes of deep fried potato. If potato is used as a substitute for the Paneer the dish is called Aloomatar – Aloo being the Hindi name for potatoes.

Esculent extras in the larder will add pizazz to your basic stocks when unexpected extra mouths need to be fed. One does not want to go overboard in this area though. Remember how Margaret Thatcher lost face when she was exposed as a hoarder. Storing foodstuffs for too long can cause botulitis and other distasteful digestive disorders. Apart from the basic dry goods that most households carry, Liz Vereker keeps most of the following things to rattle up short order feasts from her closet.

L̦IZ VEREKER'S STORE CUPBOARD EXTRAS

- Pasta, noodles and brown rice.
- Extra virgin olive oil, raspberry and Balsamic vinegars, cooking sherry, mushroom ketchup.
- Tinned tomatoes, sun-dried tomatoes, tomato sauce, tomato purée.
- Mayonnaise, lemon juice, honey, pesto, Parmesan, soy sauce, teriyaki.
- Gelatine, cornflour, arrowroot.
- Sunflower seeds (to dry fry for salads), pine kernels, olives, dried mushrooms.
- Boudoir champagne biscuits, green cocktail cherries, crystallised violets and rose petals.
- *Chocolat menier*, Toblerone, vanilla sugar.
- Sultanas, muscatel raisins.
- Tinned soups which can be 'lifted' with cream, sherry, croutons etc. such as: carrot and butterbean, onion and chickpea, lobster, pheasant, tomato etc.
- Consommé, for hot or jellied soups and mousses.
- Packets of prawn crackers and poppadoms.
- Tinned guavas, tinned peaches.
- Jars of cockles and mussels in brine, anchovies.
- Tinned artichoke hearts, asparagus spears, chestnuts puréed and whole.
- Truffles whole or in pieces in jars.

The freezer can be a useful fall-back area too. With a well-stocked freezer one should be able to withstand a siege. Apart from the ordinary family basics, the following extras should assuage many appetites.

FREEZER EXTRAS

- Stock, made from chicken, ham, fish or vegetables, frozen in ice trays to be used as required, one cube or more at a time.
- Fresh herbs such as basil, French tarragon (not Russian), summer savoury, cardamons, mint, parsley, etc. etc. Stored in plastic bags, these can be crumbled directly from frozen into sauces, marinades or other dishes as required.
- Filo pastry, puff pastry, vol-au-vent cases.
- Sliced pan (for a quick melba toast).
- Brioches, which can be served plain or filled with paté or mousse or used as a base for savouries.
- Packets of stewed apple for strudel, with muscatels as a crumble or as a sauce for pork dishes.
- Raspberries, loganberries cranberries, gooseberries, red, white and black currants.
- Skinned chicken-breast fillets and barbary duck breast fillets for a quick main course.
- Vanilla ice-cream, for dressing up in a hundred ways.
- Ready stuffed pancakes frozen in individual portions.
- Whole-boned baby guinea fowl stuffed with apricots. Even joints of wild boar and bison are available here now.
- Oven ready snails in garlic butter, frogs' legs (right and left), *Rougie foie gras*, breast of *Magret* goose, quail *en croute*, smoked venison and other goodies which can lift any occasion out of the ordinary.

Sometimes an unexpected, or even expected, guest will arrive with a handsome present of food. This can be a problem for the hostess who is expected to process it to table stage if she does not have the equipment, or worse, the expertise to cook the dish in the classic manner. A heroic salmon can become a nightmare if you do not have a similarly sized fish kettle. Even if you have one fish kettle the necessity to produce half a dozen of them would probably defeat most people. Matty Ryan solves this problem by cooking shoals of fish simultaneously in the dishwasher. He has, on occasions, fed up to eighty people at a time using five or six mammoth fish. Oddly enough this solution to such a problem is not entirely contemporary. Brillat-Savarin, arriving at a house where his host and hostess were at odds over the cooking of an enormous turbot, devised a sort of cradle in which he could steam the beast over the wash copper.

Matty's more modern method is as follows:

MATTY RYAN'S CHINA WASH SALMON

For each washed up salmon melt two to three ounces of butter with lemon juice and herbs.

Brush and baste the salmon thoroughly inside and out and then wrap each one in three separate layers of foil, ensuring that the seams do not overlap at any point and that the wrapping is entirely waterproof. Make sure that the foil is not punctured as the fish are laid in the dishwasher.

Switch on the china wash cycle. In most machines this lasts for about 55 minutes and rises to a maximum temperature of 65°C.

After the fish have been taken out of the machine leave them to rest for a minimum of one hour before unwrapping and serving.

The foil will preserve their heat if you are planning a hot dish. If you intend to serve them cold they can rest as long as is convenient.

A few other of Matty's impromptu concoctions which taste sensational are:

STORE CUPBOARD SALMON RAMEKINS
(6-8 for starters)

1 large tin salmon, boned and skinned

1 packet bread sauce

Breadcrumbs

A little grated cheese

Make up the bread sauce according to directions and mix through it the boned and skinned salmon.

Divide the mixture between small ramekin dishes and top with a mixture of grated cheese and breadcrumbs.

Brown under the grill and serve with lemon wedges – five minutes! A little parsley scattered over them can give the appearance of hours of dedicated work in the kitchen.

TROPICAL TOMATO SOUP
(serves 8)

3 tins good quality tomato soup

1 large tin grapefruit segments

1 large glass of sherry

Liquidise the grapefruit segments and stir into the tomato soup.

Heat up and add the sherry.

You will not believe the difference.

If you adore commercial vanilla ice-cream you might not approve of gilding the lily. If, on the other hand, you feel it lacks character you might like to try:

CORNER SHOP CASSATA

(serves about 6, depending on enthusiasm)

1 block vanilla ice-cream

2 Crunchy bars

Honey

Whiskey

Coarsely crush the Crunchy bars. Let the ice-cream soften a little and stir in the chunks. Refreeze.

Meanwhile melt equal quantities of honey and whiskey together over a low heat, allowing about one tablespoonful each of whiskey and honey for each person.

Another version of this almost instant pudding is to substitute some chopped marshmallows, muscatel raisins and chocolate chips for the whiskey sauce.

Not all culinary emergencies are caused by third parties. Burns and scalds can happen in any kitchen. A packet of frozen peas makes a wonderful ice-pack for a burn. If you do not have this an effective old Afghan remedy is to halve a potato and hold the cut edge against the burnt skin for ten minutes or so.

Some of the tips that have been passed on to me are, sadly, only of academic interest to my own lifestyle. I am told, for example, that if you need to roast an extra chicken quickly to cope with an unexpected influx the cooking time can be halved by stuffing the body cavity with flatware. The heavier the weight of the spoons and forks the quicker the results. This tip only works if the silver is solid sterling. Plate simply won't do. I find it hard enough to stretch my decent silver round a table setting without diverting half a dozen items into a kitchen aid, but I can vouch for the efficacy of a clean four inch nail driven through a baked potato which shares the same thermal principle.

Similarly, since all wines seem to dematerialise very quickly in my own household, I have not yet personally put this advice from Max Hastings of the *Daily Telegraph* to the test:

'If, like me, you have a damp cellar, spray labels of your wine bottles with hair lacquer before putting them in the racks. This will remove from your wife any excuse, a year or two down the line, for giving the Leoville Barton '82 to the local bazaar on the grounds that she had no means of knowing that it was not a Rioja.'

On a more mundane plane, I can personally guarantee that an apparently terminally wilted lettuce can be revived by soaking in water to which a lump of coal has been added for a few hours.

Feeding family and friends on a self-catering holiday can produce an entirely different set of hazards. Rented houses hardly ever have food processors and the saucepans are generally sparse and nasty. I always take at least two favourite, sharp knives; a large one for carving and a small one for chopping. A spatula, a wooden spoon and a whisk go into the luggage too. It is amazing how irritating the lack of one of these simple items can be. I take my own reliable openers for cans, wine and crown caps along with a garlic crusher, a plastic orange squeezer, a sieve, a few skewers and a tongs. A decent pair of scissors can come in handy for all those nail-breaking packets with little arrows saying 'tear here'. An empty bottle can double as a rolling pin and a hairdryer can be substituted, to a great extent, for a *bain-marie.* Butter, chocolate and other things can be melted in any bowl or sauce boat with the flow of hot air

If the Gîte has no suitable pan for cooking fish such as sole or plaice, they can be ironed with an ordinary domestic iron between a double thickness of baking parchment. Iron them gently for about three or four minutes each side depending on the size of the fish and the efficiency of the iron.

Another useful extra is string. It is never provided in rented properties and has a thousand uses from trussing joints to opening wine. If you find yourself without a corkscrew or a cork breaks off in a bottle, simply press the cork down firmly until it is floating below the neck. Make a loop of string and insert it into the bottle, manoeuvering it until the cork is sitting upright in the loop of string. Draw the cork upwards until it is positioned in line with the neck of the bottle and give a very sharp tug. Once you have mastered this technique it works like magic every time. I first saw this trick demonstrated many years ago by Hugh of the late lamented Snaffles Restaurant.

My first rule for keeping my sanity on a self-catering holiday is to keep everything as simple as possible. My second is to have an adoring male with a platinum credit card or two. If he is otherwise engaged it is a good idea to devise cunning ways of getting other people enthusiastically involved in the food process. Some primal instinct seems to ensure that people get greater enjoyment from food which they have foraged themselves. Young nettles, blackberries, mushrooms, mackerel and all kinds of small molluscs aquire a greater savour when they are free. Most seaside cottages in this country are not far from a mussel bed, and once the gathering has been done, cooking them is simplicity itself.

Moules à la Marinière

4 pints mussels

1 bottle of dry white wine (preferably a Muscadet)

4 shallots (or one small onion) finely chopped

3-4 oz butter

Parsley, thyme and bay-leaf

Wash, scrape and beard the mussels.

Put parsley, thyme and bay-leaf into a pot with the chopped shallots. Add mussels and 1 ounce of butter cut into small pieces.

Pour in the wine and cook, covered over a high heat until all the mussels are open. (Discard any which remain closed at this stage.)

Take the mussels from the pot and remove the top shell from each one.

Keep them hot while removing the herbs from the cooking liquor and discarding.

Add the remaining butter to the stock with freshly ground black pepper, and heat until slightly reduced.

Pour this sauce over the mussels and sprinkle with freshly chopped parsley.

Epicurean emergencies should never induce the paralysis of despair. Always remember that many of the world's great dishes were the result of ghastly mistakes or sheer desperation. Chicken Marengo, first served at Napoleon's victory feast after the battle of Marengo, was the unlikely but successful marriage of the only comestibles which his cook could rustle up in a war-devastated countryside.

CHICKEN À LA MARENGO
This method comes from Larousse Gastronomique *and serves four.*

Joint and sauté a chicken in oil. Dilute the pan juices with half a cup of white wine then add one cup of rich thickened veal gravy and a crushed clove of garlic.

Cook over a high heat for a few minutes and strain.

Put the chicken on a dish.

Garnish it with 8 mushrooms, which you have previously sautéed with the chicken, 4 very small fried eggs (bantams are ideal) or just the yokes of 4 larger eggs, 4 large crayfish, 4 heart-shaped croutons fried in butter.

Sprinkle with chopped parsley and decorate with 8 sliced truffles if you wish.

Of course I'm not suggesting you dive on the children's hamsters or chase the King Charles around the kitchen when half the office lands on your doorstep at closing time. A copy of *Consuming Passions* and a cool head are the ingredients which will get you through the culinary crisis.

Tomorrow is Another Diet

'When your waist is busted your bust is wasted.'
Anon.

*Warning: This chapter could seriously
improve your health.
If like me, you tend to eschew self-flagellation
skip the next few pages and go straight to the next chapter.*

I am never obsessed by the next meal unless I am on holiday or on a diet. It seems that the best way to lose weight is to become so focused on another issue that food and calorie counting are completely forgotten. In my experience an unhappy love affair is a sure way of shedding the kilos – hit the vodka, exhaust yourself by weeping copiously and boring your friends rigid. Try it for three days and, as the ad says, see the weight fall off. Failing that you could take Roz Lawrence's advice, namely 'get the 'flu or go to Egypt'.

There are less drastic solutions for those occasions when you feel that a little less of you will make more impact. Rigid regimes of lettuce leaves and lemon tea are only for the very highly disciplined and not for this sybarite. I am an all or nothing girl and would prefer the short, sharp shock of a fast any time. I choose a few days when I'm not too pressured but have lots of gentle distractions around me. For 48 hours I drink gallons of water and eat nothing then go gently back on to fruit and vegetables the next day. It is a great way to cleanse the system as well as shedding a few pounds.

Bronwyn Conroy, whose sleek appearance speaks for itself, recommends this two day fast:

BRONWYN CONROY'S FAST
(2 days)

FOR 2 SUCCESSIVE DAYS:

First thing in the morning – a glass of hot water with the juice of half a lemon.

Mid-morning – a glass of mineral water with a slice of lemon.

Lunch time – lemon tea.

Mid-afternoon – a glass of mineral water with a slice of lemon.

Dinner – a glass of tomato juice with a slice of lemon.

This fast has an instant effect on the waistline and completely detoxifies the system.

Bronwyn advises keeping busy without doing anything too strenuous. Take your mind off the rumbling within by going to a theatre, a concert or a film.

Bronwyn, whose beauty advice is valued by most of Ireland's household names, also suggests carrying a few bananas round in one's bag when on a diet. When the pangs of hunger become unbearable or the energy levels drop, unzip one rather than succumbing to chocolate cravings; Mary Finan swears by it too. If you are on an alcohol free regime and you come home after a hard day at the office with your tongue hanging out for that glass of vino or a cool G & T, turn the glass of water that you are allowed into a more glamorous experience by using a pretty glass, aerated water, ice, a squeeze of lemon juice, a dash of angostura and a slice of lime. Psychologically it really works, I'm told.

Two other dishes she recommends for keeping the inches and the pangs at bay are:

Bronwyn Conroy's Low Calorie Soup

1 large courgette

2 medium carrots

3 beef tomatoes

Generous sprig of mint

1 clove garlic, chopped

1 vegetable stock cube

3/4 pint water

Roughly chop the vegetables and cook all the ingredients together for 20 minutes.

Remove the mint stalk but retain the leaves.

Blend all the ingredients in an electric blender.

Bronwyn Conroy's Cucumber Dip

1/2 thinly sliced cucumber

1 carton natural yoghurt

Grated rind of 1 lemon

Juice of 1/2 a lemon

1 clove garlic, crushed

Black pepper

Blend all these ingredients in an electric blender and use to enliven *crudités*.

She also suggests that a light, low calorie mayonnaise should be kept at hand to be eaten as it is, or flavoured with garlic or lemon, for those who really cannot survive without sauces.

When my life flashes past on my death bed I am quite sure that I will remember the gorgeous meals I have eaten rather than the diets I have endured. Still, it is pleasant, if one has been having too much of the good life to find a dish that has damage limitation and is still delicious. Joan Collins, who has a figure most of her contemporaries would die(t) for swears by this simple broccoli dish.

JOAN COLLINS' BROCCOLI SALAD

Broccoli florets

Cauliflower florets

Cherry tomatoes

Flaked toasted almonds

For dressing:

1 tbsp fresh tarragon

1 tbsp wine vinegar

1 tbsp lemon juice

1 tbsp orange juice

½ tsp balsamic vinegar

1 clove garlic

1 tsp Dijon mustard

1 tsp castor sugar

Mixed, chopped herbs to taste

Steam the broccoli and cauliflower florets until they are just *al dente*.

Be careful not to overcook and lose the crunchy texture.

The cauliflower might take a little longer to reach this stage.

Allow them to cool.

Halve the cherry tomatoes and toss them through the broccoli and cauliflower then sprinkle the toasted almonds on top.

Mix the dressing either by putting all the ingredients in a Magimix or by shaking them up well in a screw-top jar.

Another of Joan's terrific maintenance recipes for girls who don't want to grow any bigger is:

JOAN COLLINS' MUSHROOM SALAD

½ lb button mushrooms	Slice the spring onions and sauté very lightly in a little of the olive oil.
4 cloves garlic	Slice the mushrooms and add them to the onions.
2 tsp ground coriander	Toss them in the olive oil for just a moment then add the garlic, coriander, cumin, salt, pepper and lemon juice.
2 tsp ground cumin	
Sea salt and fresh ground pepper	Moisten with the remaining olive oil, chill well and serve garnished with the chopped mint and parsley.
1 bunch of scallions	
5 tbsp olive oil	
Lemon juice to taste	
Chopped parsley and mint to garnish	

I've done my time at Champneys and Forest Mere. There's no question that a week in either establishment re-educates the palate and revives the body. One of the best tips that I picked up at Champneys was substituting spicy Bovril for endless cups of tea and coffee with the inevitable biscuits.

CHAMPNEYS' SPICY BOVRIL

Put 1 teaspoon of Bovril, 1 teaspoon of pure lemon juice, 1 drop of tabasco sauce, a dash of Worcester sauce and fresh pepper into a mug and stir in boiling water, for a very nourishing, low-calorie drink.

However disciplined you are about your appearance there are always occasions when you will want to look that little bit better than your best; watching your daughter walk up the aisle, meeting up with old school friends or seeing ex-lovers. When panic strikes a few days ahead of one of these outings reach for Miranda Iveagh's 48 hour diet which will guarantee a reduced midriff. It has been known to dissolve 2 or 3 inches in 48 hours and we have both been using it since the 'sixties.

MIRANDA IVEAGH'S MIDRIFF MINIMISER

Your daily rations, the same on both days, are:
• 2 eggs
• 2 oranges
• 1 pint milk

You can vary the way you eat these items, for example on the first day you might have orange juice for breakfast, hard-boiled eggs for lunch and hot milk in the evening.

On the second day you can vary it with a coddled egg for breakfast, a raw egg beaten up in milk at midday and two segmented oranges for supper, and so forth.

The strange thing is that, as diets go, it does not seem at all boring at the time and it is tremendously effective.

GILL'S MIRACLE DIET

In a desperate last ditch attempt to lose weight for one of my daughter's weddings, I followed this assiduously for ten days and lost just over half a stone. As Gill Bowler said to me, 'This is a diet and not, I repeat NOT, a Lourdes cure.' Maybe not, but it certainly had some miraculous properties for me.

The two fastest ways to lose weight are (i) to cut out all fat and (ii) to cut out salt. Forget about the health angle, these two things are guaranteed to give the fastest possible weight loss and probably work better than fasting, which only slows down the metabolic rate.

Fat means not just butter and milk but all cheeses except cottage, all yoghurts, except very low fat branded ones. It also means no pastry, biscuits, chocolate, coconut, nuts, cooking oils and mayonnaise. The reason fat-free or low cholesterol diets work is because they cut out the high calorific foods, and all the things that make food taste nice. Which brings me to salt. Salt aids fluid retention, gives one an appetite, and generally makes food taste better – no salt, no desire to eat!

Cut out all tinned and processed foods except fruit. Cut out Bovril, Marmite, sauces, smoked foods, bacon, sausages, crisps. All the obvious foods as well as packaged cereals (the only exception being Shredded Wheat). Limit yourself to four slices of bread per day.

Allow yourself $1/3$ pint skimmed or $1/4$ pint semi-skimmed milk, $1/2$ bottle wine, or 2 Gins, diet tonic or alternative.

DAY 1

Breakfast: Grilled tomatoes, mushrooms, toast.

Lunch: Omelette and French Bread.

Dinner: Leg of lamb, steak or chargrilled escalope of veal, vegetables, potato.

DAY 2

Breakfast: Shredded Wheat.

Lunch: Penne/Pasta and fresh tomato sauce.

Dinner: Grilled sole, broccoli, new potatoes.

DAY 3

Breakfast: Poached egg on toast.

Lunch: Fruit platter i.e. melon, oranges, pineapple, berries.

Dinner: Grilled breast of chicken (no skin) mushrooms, tomatoes, baked potato.

DAY 4

Breakfast: Banana, toast or wholemeal bread.

Lunch: Fresh salmon and cucumber sandwich.

Dinner: Fillet steak, sweet and sour onions, peas, baked potato with low fat yoghurt and chives.

DAY 5

Breakfast: Boiled egg, toast.

Lunch: Home-made vegetable soup (no salt) or pears with cottage cheese.

Dinner: Curried lamb (no salt), rice, fresh fruit salad.

DAY 6

Breakfast: Melon, toast.

Lunch: Fillet beef, salade nicoise.

Dinner: Roast turbot, puréed carrots/parsnips, spinach, new potatoes.

DAY 7

Breakfast: Scrambled egg, tomato, mushrooms.

Lunch: Baguette filled with lettuce, cucumber, tomatoes and scallions.

Dinner: Roast leg of lamb, tomatoes provençal, green beans, boiled or baked potatoes. Baked apple, low fat yoghurt.

One of the real thoroughbreds among the racy set of this country is Vi Lawlor. Despite her champagne lifestyle she is lean and finely honed. Dancing till dawn most days of the week probably works off some of the effects of the Dom Perignon but I have always suspected that she had another secret weapon in the war most women wage against the kilos.

A few years ago we were in the Monaco Sports Club in Monte Carlo and she was as lissom as the best of them. I was not. In a great spirit of camaraderie she shared her secret with me. It should remove 7 pounds in a week.

VI LAWLOR'S DIET
(1 week)

DAY 1: All kinds of fruit and as much as you want except bananas.

DAY 2: All kinds of vegetables and a large baked potato with lettuce.

DAY 3: Fruit and vegetables (no bananas, sweetcorn, dried beans or potatoes).

DAY 4: Up to 8 bananas and $1/2$ pint skimmed milk.

DAY 5: Beef with tomatoes. Have as much as you like, prepared in any way that you choose. Drink at least 3 glasses of water.

DAY 6: Beef and vegetables (excluding sweetcorn, dried beans or potatoes).

DAY 7: Brown rice, vegetables and unsweetened fruit juice.

SOUP SUPPLEMENT

*During this diet you can eat the following soup as often
as you like. There are no restrictions on quantity,
in fact it helps the weight loss.*

½ *white cabbage*

1 onion

3 or 4 carrots

1 green pepper

2 or 3 sticks celery

*1 small tin of
tomatoes or* ¾ *lb
fresh ones*

*1*½ *vegetable stock
cubes*

*1*½ *pints water*

Simmer all these ingredients until cooked and
then blend in an electric blender.

No salt is allowed on this diet.

Vegetables can be raw, steamed or simmered.

Black coffee and black tea are allowed as are
sugar free wafers.

Vanity and aesthetics are not the only reasons why people
need to lose weight in a hurry. Actresses and models can
have urgent, financial inducements for keeping in shape,
as Maria Fitzgerald has. Maria is a licensed amateur jockey,
owner and private trainer. She often finds it necessary to
shed 8-10 pounds at quite short notice to reach her riding
weight but while doing so she needs to maintain and,
ideally, increase her level of fitness. As races are
advertised about three weeks before the off, this is the
time-scale she uses for losing about half a stone.

MARIA FITZGERALD'S PROGRAMME

WEEK 1

Maria describes the first week as one of mental programming. She does not alter her normal, healthy diet in any way but she slightly reduces the quantity of food that she eats. She steps up her level of exercise but basically this is the week when she gets psyched up for the big push.

WEEK 2

She now adds a 3 mile run or an additional aerobic session to her normal routine of riding out each morning and doing some aerobics in the evening. She also cuts down on her food intake but at no point in her weight loss programme does she cut out fat, which she feels is an essential catalyst for the fat soluble vitamins, A,D,E,& K. Carbohydrate stays too, for energy.

A typical day's food in Week 2 would be;

Breakfast: A good multi vitamin pill, a glass of fruit juice, muesli with skimmed milk or two slices of brown bread with butter, tea or coffee with skimmed milk.

Mid morning: Tea or coffee, a piece of fruit or a diet yoghurt for energy.

Lunch: Steamed vegetables with a potato and a few slices of lean meat or fish, or a good mixed salad with a low calorie dressing.

Mid afternoon: Tea or coffee, fruit or diet yoghurt.

6 p.m: A carbohydrate snack, toasted sandwich or scone, for energy.

After this Maria eats nothing more although she might take a cup of tea or coffee and invariably takes some exercise.

WEEK 3

The horse is entered six days before the race so, at this point, there is no turning back and the objectives of the weighing in room have to be achieved now or never. The previous week's eating routine stays in place, with quantities being cut down a little more and some reduction on the fat intake. A second three mile run is added to her exercise programme and the evening aerobic session may be lengthened.

Maria stresses that her mental condition is the key to her success in these blitzes. During the entire three week period she drinks no alcohol. Initially she finds that her energy level drops a little, but it is well back to normal by the end of the second week. With her exercise programme in addition to her diet she is riding a winner by the end of the third week. It is important to stress that before embarking on any of these diets you should consult a doctor.

I suppose we have all fallen of the wagon now and then, but a slender gourmet is still an attainable dream rather than an oxymoron. Luckily for me many of my best loved foods – frozen figs, oysters, salads – are not fattening, but all drinks, with the happy exception of Champagne, are. Dieting girlfriends also swear by the new style German Trocken dry wines with their elegant flavour. They are low in sugar and alcohol and they age as well as my girlfriends! Anyway, I think that nowadays, we worry too much about the 'perfect' figure and certainly, after forty I would rather have a face than a figure. And, believe me, after forty that's your choice.

A Few of my Favourite Things

*'Give me the luxuries of life and
I will willingly do without the necessities.'*
Frank Lloyd Wright.

A little of what you fancy might not always do you good but it can certainly give you a kick. I think that it is important, in this politically correct, polyunsaturated era to stick up for what you enjoy. Forbidden fruits have always done more for my complexion than nut cutlets and tofu. On principle I always say yes to *foie gras*, Beluga or Dom because spoiling makes me feel valued but, deep down, I am a simple girl who enjoys comforting, traditional fare just as much as the luxuries.

My favourite dish – apart from Daniel Day Lewis – is spaghetti bolognese. Unless I have it at least twice a week I get withdrawal symptoms. In fact, spaghetti bolognese is the principal reason why I could never embrace vegetarianism. Listing the memorable meals I have eaten during my life would fill another book but they all had one thing in common – the pleasure of making or cementing friendships over good food and fine drink. Food is such a wonderful catalyst in human relationships that my memories of special dishes are inextricably intertwined with the companions who shared them.

If I had to single out one meal that I would like to have again, unchanged in all respects, it would be a repast of grilled sardines, fresh from the sea, served on the deck of a schooner in the Mediterranean by the man I love. Contrary to my image I have always believed that, in matters aesthetic, simplicity is the essence of style.

Like most women I have had a mass of different motives on the menu when feeding others. I've prepared meals to impress, to cajole, to seduce, to soothe, to cosset and to nurture. I have stood over the stove as a daughter, a wife, a mother, a lover, a hostess and, perhaps most importantly, as a working woman who still likes to see her family gathered round the table sharing a meal.

Perhaps that is why so many simple basics rank high on my list of best-loved foods. Family favourites such as bangers and mash, prawn cocktail and Welsh rarebit may not rank high in the designer grub category but they are all full of happy associations for me. I don't know when the Welsh laid claim to the rarebit but in 1859 Alexis Soyer published this familiar sounding recipe under the title 'Irish Rarebit'.

ALEXIS SOYER'S IRISH RAREBIT

4 oz grated cheese
2 tsp flour
1/2 cup butter
1 chopped gherkin
1 tsp mustard powder
3 tbsp stout or ale

Mix the flour and butter in a small saucepan over a low heat.
Add all the other ingredients except the gherkin and cook slowly to a thick paste, then add the chopped pickle.
Spread it onto toast that has been cooked on one side only and brown under grill.
This mixture can also be put into a bun with the crumb removed and baked in the oven for about 10 or 15 minutes.

The prawn cocktail has had a chequered history here. For years, along with the well-done sirloin steak, the French fries and the apple pie *à-la-mode* it was the apotheosis of the Irish night out. Then it became smart to see it as naff until I reinstated it as the ultimate prelude to a delicious dinner. It should be served in roomy, glamorous glasses – Georgian rummers are ideal – and never attempt it with frozen fish. Put a layer of very finely shredded iceberg lettuce in the base of each glass and top with about 4 ounces of the biggest, juiciest, freshest prawns you can find. Garnish each portion with chopped parsley and a lemon wedge. I know that some people do not share my unashamed impartiality for Marie-Rose dressing so I hand it around separately. I make it the quick and easy way by mixing Hellman's mayonnaise with tomato purée, lemon juice, Worcester sauce and tabasco to taste.

Old fashioned nursery food like bangers and mash can be given a facelift with some of the excellent continental sausages on sale now. The coarse-cut Bratwurst sausages of beef and pork are particularly good in this simple dish.

BRATWURST RAGOUT
(serves 4)

1 lb Bratwurst sausages	Cut the sausages into 1½ inch pieces and cook with the tomatoes in an oiled frying pan over a medium heat for 10 minutes stirring occasionally.
1 tin tomatoes, coarsely cut	
1 lb fresh French beans	Add all the French beans and continue cooking for a further 5 minutes.
	Serve with creamed potatoes or crusty french bread.

Another long-cherished indulgence is a sinful calorie overload of afternoon tea. Whether it is served under a beech tree on a summer lawn or by a crackling applewood fire in December dusk it breathes of a bygone age of leisure and grace. It is a world away from the bustle of a newspaper office and the tyranny of the telephone. A proper tea should outrage every dietary shibboleth and should be consumed in a spirit of sublime decadence.

The handsomest tea pot you can lay your hands on should be filled with Lapsang Souchong, Earl Grey or best Darjeeling. The china should be as thin as possible and anything hot should be served in one of those squat, two-storey muffin dishes with hot water in the base. Teatime sandwiches should be entirely frivolous and bear no resemblance to the sustenance that people take out in lunch boxes.

THE CUCUMBER SANDWICH

Cucumber	Peel the desired amount of cucumber and slice very thinly on a mandoline.
Brown Bread	
(Hovis or similar)	Sprinkle with a little salt and put aside in a colander to sweat.
Butter	
Fresh dill	Soften 2 or 3 ounces of butter with a dessertspoonful of fresh dill and pound in your
A sardine or two	filleted sardines.

Cut the bread as thinly as possible, spreading the flavoured butter on each slice before cutting, (an electric carving knife can be useful here).

Pat the cucumber slices dry on kitchen paper and make up the sandwiches. Remove the crusts and cut into triangles.

This recipe for toasts from Melosine Bowes-Daly's Swahili and English cookery book makes a good filler for the muffin dish.

CINNAMON TOASTS

Cut a stale loaf in slices and remove the crusts.

Dip one side of each slice in a mixture of sherry and beer and leave to dry, then dip the toasts in cream, well seasoned with nutmeg and cinnamon and fry in very hot, clarified butter until golden brown on both sides. Sift with sugar and serve with a side dish of whipped cream, flavoured with a little sherry.

At least one kind of cake is an essential part of the ceremonial. This one is beautifully sticky and is even more delicious spread with rich, farmhouse butter.

DATE AND WALNUT LOAF

8 oz chopped dates

4 oz vanilla sugar

1 tsp bicarbonate of soda

1 pinch salt

2 oz butter

2 oz walnuts

8 oz self-rising flour

1 beaten egg

6 fl oz water

Cut the butter into small pieces and place in a bowl with the dates, sugar, salt and bicarbonate of soda.

Boil the water and mix in, stirring until all the butter has melted.

Let the mixture cool a little and then add the beaten egg, chopped walnuts and, finally, the sifted self-raising flour.

Line the base of a 2 lb loaf tin with butter paper and grease well.

Cook in a moderate oven, 325°F/Gas 3, for about an hour and a quarter.

I am not a great devotee of the sliced pan, but I do feel that the best thing about its invention was the fact that it made it so easy for us all to make melba toast which I can eat anytime, any place, with absolutely everything. Making it is simplicity itself. A good excuse for a mountain of melba is chicken liver paté which is equally good hot or cold.

MELBA TOAST

Toast a slice of ordinary white sliced white pan until it is just lightly tanned on both sides. Cut off the crusts and slide a sharp knife down through the crumb between the two toasted faces so that you have two very thin pieces of bread, each one toasted on one side only.

Put these under the grill, untoasted side upwards until they curl a little and are crisp and lightly coloured. Continue this process until greed is satisfied.

CHICKEN LIVER PATÉ

6 oz chicken livers

3/4 oz breadcrumbs

1 tbsp softened butter

1 clove garlic

8 fl oz milk

2 egg yolks

Salt and pepper

Pinch of nutmeg

Pre-heat the oven to 325°F/Gas 3 and grease small moulds or ramekins with butter.

Put the livers, milk, egg yolks and garlic into a blender or food processor and blend for one minute.

Season with nutmeg, salt and pepper and sieve, then add the breadcrumbs. Pour the mixture into the moulds or ramekins and place in a roasting tin.

Pour in a sufficient amount of hot water to reach three quarters of the way up the outside of the moulds.

Cook in the oven until they are set firmly (about twenty minutes) then turn out onto small plates.

Use the caper sauce if you are serving them warm and the cranberry version if you prefer them chilled.

CAPER SAUCE

2 shallots

8 oz thick cream

2 tbsp capers

2 tbsp butter

4 oz dry white wine

Salt and pepper

Drain and chop the capers.

Chop the shallots and sweat them in the butter. Pour in the wine and cook until reduced to almost nothing.

Add the cream and the capers and stir over a low heat until the sauce has the consistency of double cream.

Pour this sauce around the paté and decorate with sprigs of fennel or edible flowers such as nasturtiums.

CRANBERRY SAUCE

1 lb cranberries

$1/2$ pint cider vinegar

$3/4$ lb white sugar

$1/4$ oz root ginger

Put the cranberries, cider vinegar and root ginger in a pan. Bring to a boil and simmer until the skins of the cranberries are just beginning to pop.

Remove the root ginger and add the sugar.

Simmer for another fifteen minutes.

Chill before serving with the cold paté.

This fruity cranberry sauce also complements one of my great loves: deep-fried Camembert.

DEEP-FRIED CAMEMBERT

*1 whole
Camembert cheese
(about 8 oz)*

Put the cheese into the freezer for about fifteen minutes to make it firm then divide it into eight equal portions.

2 tsp plain flour

*2 oz dried
breadcrumbs*

Beat the egg with the breadcrumbs then roll each section of cheese first in the flour then in the egg and breadcrumb mixture.

1 egg

6 sprigs of parsley

Deep-fry the cheese sections until they are golden. This should not take longer than 45 seconds.

Deep-fry the sprigs of parsley very quickly and use one to garnish each section of cheese.

In fact, cheese in all its delicious, different varieties is something that I would find hard to live without. One of the most delightful things about cheese is that there are always new and pleasurable discoveries to be made. I adore browsing through the cheese department in Fauchon in the Place de la Madeleine – it is one of those places where a not entirely foreign mood of sublime self-indulgence possesses me – but I'm proud of our own Irish cheeses too. Just recently I discovered that Milleens and Gubeens acquire a glorious honeyed flavour when accompanied by a modest Sauternes. I love putting an interesting cheeseboard together to conclude a fine dinner but cheese can make a delicious prelude to a meal as well. This featherlight starter illustrates perfectly the subtle appeal of cheese as an appetiser.

GRUYÈRE ROULADE

2 tbsp Parmesan cheese

2 oz fresh wholemeal breadcrumbs

6 oz grated Gruyère cheese

¼ pint cream

4 eggs, separated

3 pinches cayenne pepper

2 tbsp warm water

Good pinch dried mustard

Salt and pepper to season

For filling

A macedoine of seasonal salad; tomatoes, mushrooms, shredded iceberg lettuce, scallions, cucumber, watercress, fresh herbs etc.

Mayonnaise

Lemon juice

Pre-heat the oven to 400°F/Gas 6 and line a swiss roll tin with greaseproof paper, lightly brushed with oil.

Mix the Gruyère cheese and the breadcrumbs, add the egg yolks, cream, mustard, cayenne, salt and pepper. If the mixture seems too dry add the water.

Whip the egg-whites until stiff and gradually fold into the cheese mixture, taking care not to knock too much air out of the mixture.

Cook in the oven until the mixture is springy to the touch and the edges have shrunk slightly away from the sides of the tin. This should take about 15 minutes. Remove from the oven and cool slightly.

Sprinkle the Parmesan on another sheet of greaseproof paper and turn the cheese mousse out onto it.

Remove the lining paper from the base of the mousse, using a palate knife and roll up the roulade lengthwise in the Parmesan sprinkled paper and then leave to cool.

Unroll the roulade carefully and spread with a light layer of mayonnaise, then top with the macedoine of salad and sprinkle with lemon juice and then re-roll. Cut the roulade into slices for serving.

No catalogue of palatable pleasures would be complete without the potable ones. As somebody once said, wine is like sex: nobody will admit to not knowing all about it. While I readily admit that I still do not know all about *wine,* I have had an excellent teacher and I've always been an enthusiastic pupil. I certainly think that wine is man's greatest invention since the wheel and, like the wheel, it helps to keep things rolling along smoothly on life's rocky path. I adore dessert wines like Château Coutet and the old, sweet Vouvrays, especially those from Gaston Huet. Vintage port such as Taylor's '66 or '77 is another great treat and I have never been known to decline champagne.

Sadly my fondness for wine means that I have never had the patience to 'put down' a collection of wines and wait for them to reach their peak of perfection. My wine rack seems to be constantly in need of replenishment. However, I asked Declan Ryan what he would advise if an unexpected windfall of £500 should come my way, with the provision that it had to be spent on wine which one was not allowed to touch for a few years. The guiding principle behind this agreeable fantasy was to go for quality rather than quantity. This was his advice:

DECLAN RYAN'S WINDFALL WINES

'The red really must be a good Cru Classe Claret. There are trendier but I like the honest style of the château owned by Irish born Anthony Barton, and if, in ten years, you prefer cashing in your investment rather than drinking it you should make a nice profit. That and a case of recent vintage Château de Pez should do nicely. Another way of laying down would be to buy relatively larger quantities of inexpensive wines from the Rhone Valley. A good Gigondas or Cornas can last 20 years or more. They will not appreciate fiancially but are fabulous wines to drink. Look out for wines from Chapoutier, Chave, Janoulet or Guigal.' What Declan describes as 'lifetime memories' are a 25-year-old Château Latour among the reds and a good Corton Charlemagne among the whites.

Other people who enterd into the spirit of the windfall game with enthusiasm suggest Bordeaux 2nd, 3rd, 4th and 5th classed growths (Crus Classes).

For example:

From PAUILLAC: Château Pichon Longueville – Baron and Chateau Lynch-Bages.

From ST. JULIEN: Château Leoville-Barton

From MARGAUX: Château Palmer and Château Kirwan.

Note: The year is important – '89 and '90, for instance, are great vintages.

Port, of course, is one of the safest wines you can buy from an investment point of view.

Like Proust with his *madeleine,* the taste of some foods can sandbag me with nostalgia for times past. My great weakness is for dishes that evoke happy memories. On a recent trip to Hydra I collected these Greek recipes which will always recall to me sunny days of compatible company beside a wine dark sea.

For me, aubergines are the sexiest vegetables – dark, rich, fleshy and polished. Their purple gloss seems to promise infinite pleasure. The Greeks must agree for they have over a thousand ways to prepare them. This recipe is special and sybaritic:

GRILLED AUBERGINES
serves 4-6

3-4 medium sized aubergines (oblong if possible) about 1½ -1¾ lb, cut lengthways into ¼ inch slices

Salt

1-2 tbsp olive oil

2 tbsp vinaigrette

1 tbsp finely chopped flat leaf parsley

1 tsp finely chopped fresh mint

Salt the slices of aubergine generously, arrange them on a large plate and weight with another plate.

Set aside for 30 minutes. Rinse them and dry between two towels, pressing well to remove bitter juice.

With a pastry brush paint the slices lightly with olive oil.

Grill for about 2 minutes on each side, so they are tender.

Serve hot, drizzled with vinaigrette, and sprinkle with parsley mixed with fresh mint.

My next Grecian indulgence might look like another excuse for using aubergine. It is, but it so happens that this Homeric stew leaves its Irish counterpart in the shade. Some like it hot with feta cheese sprinkled on top but it's gorgeous cold with a dollop of indigenous yoghurt.

VEGETABLE STEW À LA GRÈCQUE
Serves 6-12

1 lb aubergine	Cube the aubergines and soak them in heavily-salted water for 30 minutes or more.
12 oz onions, sliced	
4 tbsp olive oil	Drain well and pat dry.
1/2 tsp sugar	In a large heavy-bottomed pot (or flameproof casserole), fry the onions in 4 tablespoons of olive oil until transparent.
8 oz red or green peppers, seeded and sliced	
	Sprinkle with sugar and caramelise them.
8 oz courgettes, sliced into rounds	Add the aubergine cubes and sauté until brown.
8 oz fresh green beans	Stir in the sliced peppers, courgettes, beans and garlic.
6 garlic cloves, chopped	Add more oil if necessary, and continue cooking at high heat, stirring frequently, for 5 minutes.
1 lb tomatoes, skinned, seeded and finely chopped	Add the chopped tomato and cook until a sauce begins to form.
4 fl oz ouzo	Then pour in the ouzo and season with bay-leaves, thyme, cinnamon, cloves, salt and pepper.
2 bay-leaves	
2 tsp fresh thyme	Simmer, covered, over a very low heat until the juices are absorbed.
1/4 tsp cinnamon	Alternatively bake the stew (transferring to an earthenware casserole or roasting tin if need be), uncovered, in an oven pre-heated to 350°F/Gas 4 for 30-40 minutes.
1/4 tsp cloves	
1/2 tsp salt	
Black pepper	Stir in the parsley and serve hot or cold.
1 oz flat leaf parsley, chopped	

I can't conceive where the phrase 'I don't give a fig' came from because as far as I'm concerned this Mediterranean fruit should be cherished and revered. I'd eat figs for breakfast, lunch and dinner if I could. Hot or cold, they are mouthwatering and this recipe for baked figs allows for both. Sprinkled with almonds and accompanied by a bowl of thick yoghurt, they keep in the refrigerator for 10 days.

BAKED FIGS
(serves 8)

24 ripe figs

2½ oz blanched almonds, slivered or chopped

2 tbsp honey

Finely grated zest of 1 lemon plus 1 tbsp juice

2 bay-leaves

2 fl oz Cognac

Spread the blanched almonds on a baking sheet and toast them in an oven pre-heated to 300°F/Gas 2 for 7-10 minutes, until lightly golden.

Put the whole figs in an ovenproof glass or earthenware casserole.

Whisk the honey, lemon juice and cognac together and pour over the figs.

Sprinkle them with the lemon zest and nestle the bay-leaves among the fruits.

Cover and bake in an oven pre-heated to 350°F/Gas 4 for 20-25 minutes.

Serve sprinkled with almonds.

The favourite things that make life loveable for me are legion but food and drink, the fuel of life and relationships, rank high. Writing this book about them has been, in many ways, like a love affair – easy to get into but hard to finish.

Anthony Burgess said in *Earthly Powers*: 'I have always, throughout my literary career, found endings excruciatingly hard,' so it is some consolation to find myself in such distinguished company. I do know, however, that all of the consuming passions described here would be worthless if they were not shared with my most consuming passion of all – the loved ones.

FOOD INDEX

PERSONALITY INDEX

WEIGHT
$1/_2$ kg = 500g

IMPERIAL MEASURES	APPROXIMATE METRIC EQUIVALENT	IMPERIAL MEASURES	APPROXIMATE METRIC EQUIVALENT
1oz	25g	2lb	900g
2oz	50g	2$1/_2$lb	1.1kg
3oz	75g	3lb	1.4kg
4oz	100-125g	3$1/_2$lb	1.6kg
5oz	150g	4lb	1.8kg
1oz	175g	4$1/_2$lb	2kg
7oz	200g	5lb	2.3kg
8oz	225g	5$1/_2$lb	2.5kg
9oz	250g	6lb	2.7kg
10oz	275g	6$1/_2$lb	3kg
11oz	300g	7lb	3.2kg
12oz	325-350g	7$1/_2$lb	3.4kg
13oz	375g	8lb	3.6kg
14oz	400g	8$1/_2$lb	3.9kg
15oz	425g	9lb	4.1kg
16oz (1lb)	450g	9$1/_2$lb	4.3kg
1lb (16oz)	450g	10lb	4.5kg
1$1/_2$lb	700g		

LIQUID CAPACITY

Imperial pint (20 fl oz) measures slightly more than $1/_2$ litre – approximately 575 millilitres (ml)
100ml = 1 litre

IMPERIAL MEASURES	APPROXIMATE METRIC EQUIVALENT
1 fl oz	25ml
2 fl oz	50ml
3 fl oz	75ml
4 fl oz	100-125ml
5 fl oz	150ml
6 fl oz	175ml
7 fl oz	200ml
8 fl oz	225ml
9 fl oz	250ml
10 fl oz ($1/_2$pt)	275-300ml
20 fl oz ($1/_2$pt)	575-600ml

OVEN TEMPERATURES

Very cool	250°F	130°C	Mark $1/_2$
	275°F	140°C	Mark 1
Cool	300°F	150°C	Mark 2
Warm	325°F	170°C	Mark 3
Moderate	350°F	180°C	Mark 4
Fairly hot	375°F	190°C	Mark 5
	400°F	200°C	Mark 6
Hot	425°F	220°C	Mark 7
Very hot	450°F	230°C	Mark 8
	475°F	240°C	Mark 9
	500°F	250°C	Mark 10

To convert Fahrenheit to Celsius or Centigrade:
subtract 32, multiply by 5, divide by 9.
To convert Celsius to Fahrenheit:
multiply by 9, divide by 5 and add 32.